DR. MARVIN C. MCMASTER

THE SEVENTH SERAPH

THE SEVENTH SERAPH

By Dr. Marvin C. McMaster

ISBN: 978-1-961677-58-6 (Paperback)

Printed in the United States of America

Published by:

info@thequippyquill.com

(302) 295-2278

Contents

Preface: Angels of Fire

Seraphim stand before the face of God. They are creatures of God's fire, his holy love that cleanses and purifies Heaven. They can move at the speed of thought and often are shown as having six wings to symbolize this quickness. No other creature can look into the creator's face- save his son. Jeshua, He can do that because he is God's word incarnate as man and is resurrected as the ruler and judge.

Shaitan (Iblis) in the Qur'an (38:23) refused to fall down and worship man as Allah had ordered saying "I am greater than him for you have made me from fire, but made him of clay." Obviously he sees man as an inferior creation!

The seven Seraphim rule over the legions of God's created servants, his angelic host, who serve as his messengers. ***Lucifer,*** known as Ha-Satan, the accuser, was God's spokesman to angel kind, who led a third of the Angels in rebellion against their creator. ***Gabriel,*** who stands at God's right hand, speaks with his voice to mankind. She announced to the Virgin Mary that she would bear God's son. As the Angel Jibril, ***Gabriella*** shared the teaching of the Qur'an with the Prophet Muhammad. Michael is God's warrior and teacher of young Angels. These three Seraphs are all mentioned in the New and Old Testaments of the Bible.

Three other Seraphim are only mentioned in Tobit and 2 Edras in the Apocrypha of the Bible. ***Raphael*** is the archangel of healing. ***Uriel*** is the archangel of inspiration and wisdom. Jeremiel is the archangel in charge of keeping the Book of the Living and the Book of the Lamb containing the names of all mankind.

The final of God's Seraphim is named throughout the Bible as the Angel of Death. He touches the life of everyone who has lived or will live on earth and prepares him or her for death and resurrection. He has many names: ***Samael, Azrael, Malik al-Maut*** or simply ***Death.*** No one looks foreword to his visit.

The sex of the various Seraphim are not discussed in the Bible, the book assigned them all masculine names. Some Popes preferred it that way.

Introduction

The first visitor of the day in the medical office of Doctor Susan Maria Fernandez was listed as Matthias Samael. Petite blond Dr. Fernandez had just opened her office after a senior residency in Psychiatry at Harvard School of Medicine. She was suffering from a shocking medical diagnosis, but soldiering on until she could get another opinion from an oncologist she knew at Boston Women's Hospital.

"What can I do to help you, Dr. Samael?" Dr. Fernandez asked looking at the impressive six-foot seven-inch tall gentleman in the three-piece brown suit. He reminded her of Ricardo Montalban from the old TV show Paradise Island she had seen in reruns.

"I need your help for a very unusual psychiatric consult and I also may be of some assistance to you in your medical problem. Can we sit down in your consulting office to discuss our mutual problems?"

"Please," Susan said gesturing Dr. Samael into her office. "Please call me Susan. Names are very important. What should I call you? Is it alright if I record our conversation?"

"Of course" said her patient. "I prefer to be called Matthias, it means God's Gift in Hebrew, and Mathew in English. However, I am not sure your recoding device will be able to record an Archangel's voice."

"A what?" the good doctor said with a grin starting to dimple her cheeks.

"An archangel, a seraphim, one who stands before the face of God. I am Dr. Matthias Mort Samael, God's Angel of Death. Please relax! I am not here professionally. I have not come to extract your soul. I truly am here seeking your help as a psychiatrist. Even angels have problems with depression and rejection by their peers. My job suffers from the same problems as your dentists and they have the highest suicide rate of any medical professional.

No one likes to go to a dentist and they subtly signal that to their doctors.

My colleagues treat me the same way. I had no idea this would happen when I took the job. Death is a necessity at the end of life and preparation for your next stage. I am simply in the extraction business helping people to move on to the next life prepared for them by their Creator. But, humans fear me more than any other angel; look at the surname they have given me. Samael means the Venom of God."

"I thought you worked for Satan," said Susan.

"You are confusing me with Abaddon, a fallen Archangel who followed Satan into exile, the one they call the Angel of the Pit. I remained loyal to Yahweh when Lucifer fell. Satan was the angel I referred to who became depressed, jealous of mankind, and went insane. It was terrible! He was my boss and best friend, but I could not follow him when he confronted the all-powerful God and was cast out of Heaven. Satan uses Abaddon as his hit man and calls him the "Angel of Death" just as humans did Heinrich Himmler in your World War II, but he is no true Angel of Death. I have been stuck with this job from the beginning of time. Life in your world is only kindergarten; when you finish your work here you are resurrected into a new life. I just release you from this body and guide you into your next life."

"I feel like the one who is going crazy!" said Dr. Susan shaking her head. "I am standing here seriously talking to a person who claimed he is the Angel of Death. What proof do you have of this amazing claim? I have had many delusional mental patients in my career, who have made claims that they were Mother Earth, Napoleon, Hitler, or even Jesus. How am I to believe you are who you say you are?

"Because I am one who can tell you about the fatal brain-stem cancer that your doctors have just diagnosed for you. The only one who can take you to Raphaella, the Archangel of Healing, who can rid you completely of this terrible curse," Matthias said. "Otherwise, I will be back here in less that six months to release you from your body and guide you on to your eternal destiny. But, if you wish, I can take you to the Healer, give you protection, and make you my companion as I travel to the periods of extraordinary times of great deaths that have haunted mankind, and to direct my under-angels in these great harvests of souls."

"If you will travel with me, treat my trauma, and comfort me, I will also offer you a way out if you can stand it no more. Once every century, I will give you a chance to go back to this very moment, with your body cleansed and your cancer cured. Of course, I will have to reverse your protection and wipe your memory of our travels. But, you will finish living out your life just as you would have if the cancer and I had never turned up in your life."

"So I will be your wife and traveling companion through time?" asked Dr. Fernandez.

"No, I can't promise you that. There is no marriage in Heaven and I am a Seraph. This image you see before you is only a construct acceptable to your eyes. I am actually a being only of spirit and energy. I have taking this form so you can see and interact with me. So, the question is, will you take me on as a patient and travel with me for a time?"

"Of course, I will. I have everything to gain and nothing to lose. Let me get my medical bag and let's go see this Archangel Raphaclla."

Chapter One
Bloom Where You Are Planted

Susan led the archangel out to the front office and locked her office door. Turning to her secretary who had just arrived she said, "Vicky, tell Mark I'm going on a lengthy private consult. Ask him if he will cover my patients until I return. Merry Christmas, if I don't get back before then." Taking Matthias' arm as they walked out of the office, she said, "O.K. What's the next step?"

Clasping her hand, the Archangel said, Hold on, we simply have to step sideways. There was a flash of color and they were somewhere else. The downtown Boston buildings and the Charles River were gone and they were in a pastoral setting with a collection of buildings scattered around the path ahead of them. "Raphaella's home is in the green two-story colonial ahead on the right. Her medical offices and surgery area are on the first floor."

"Is this going to hurt," Susan asked. "I'm a bit of a coward about pain."

"I have no idea," Matthias said. "Let's go talk to her." They walked up the lane, opened the gate in the white picket fence, and knocked on the door, which swung open in greeting.

"Coming in, coming in," said a sweet voice from off to the left. "I have been expecting you. I'm in the kitchen."

They passed under an archway into a country kitchen with gleaming copper bottom pots and pans hanging on the wall. There was a massive fireplace on the far wall and a black pot was hanging on the hob filled with a bubbling stew. Water bubbled on the cast iron range on the left wall and steam filled that side of the kitchen. “You're just in time, Mort!” Said the beautiful cook with her mahogany hair pulled up into a knot on the back of her head. “Dinner is just ready. Sit down. Sit down. We'll get right down to business. I hope you like lamb and onion stew, it's my specialty. I'm Raphaella, by the way. Have a piece of pie.”

“Raphaella, this is Dr. Susan Fernandez. She is my consulting psychiatrist who is traveling with me on my assignment. She asks to be called Susan. I brought her here to see if you can cure her of her cancer.” Matthias said.

The table was set for four, there was steaming black bread fresh from the oven, freshly churned butter, and strawberry jam on the table, and glasses of chilled milk. “Uriel will be joining us in a few minutes. He had a conference to attend with the boss. Now about this cancer that is bothering you, Susan. How long ago did you begin to feel symptoms? Is there pain and where exactly is it located?"

“It started with headaches on both sides of my forehead about six months ago. They got so bad that I would have to go to bed when the light show began. Then the pain moved to the back of my neck about a month ago and it was terrible. My massage therapist could do nothing about it and sent me to an Orthopod.

Two weeks ago it began to affect my swallowing. I would yawn, I would get pains in both sides of my neck and I couldn’t swallow. With massage eventually it would clear, but it sent me to a Neurologist and eventually to an Oncologist, who last week ran an MRI and found this mass on my spinal column under my mid-brain,” said Susan “The Oncologist told me the cancer mass was growing fast, was inoperable, and would kill me with terrible pain in six months even if I was living on morphine. And then Matthias showed up and promised me a cure and I grabbed it with both hands. I don't want to die.”

"I certainly don't blame you for that. Eat your stew while I cut the pie." The stew was delicious and the berry pie was out of this world.

Finally, Susan said, "Shouldn't we get started on a treatment? I have screwed up my courage up to the sticking point, but I can only take so much pain before I pass out."

"Are you hurting?" ask Raphaella. "Turn your neck. Bend your head foreword and back. Try and yawn while you nod forward. How does it feel? Let me look at the back of your neck." Raphaella poked and prodded gently, smiled and said, "You can relax. You are cured. I'm sure that the mass is gone and it won't be back. The cure was in the stew. I can give you some sugar pills or a shot or two if it will make you feel better, but you are a fully healthy twenty-five year old young woman."

"What? That's all there is too it? No pain? How wonderful! You are a marvel, Raphaella. How can I ever thank, ever repay you?" Susan said leaning over to kiss the Seraph on the cheek.

"You can't. Praise the Lord God. He is the source of all healing, miracles, and good things we enjoy. I am simply his tool in this miracle. Go with Mort and minister to him with all your training and insight," Raphaella said with a smile. "Hello, darling. How did the meeting go with the Lord Almighty" Another tall blond Angel came into the kitchen looking like a young Viking berserker.

"We got everything worked out on Earth for another week. Put a couple more plates on the table, I brought Michael and Gabriella home for supper. I invited Jeremiel, but he had to scurry off and update his books on the meeting." Raphaella gestured at the table and two more chairs and dinner settings appeared as the table stretched to accommodate them. "Jeshua said he would stop over later for chess. Hi, Mort. Hello Susan, how are you settling into your practice?" The blond giant bent and kissed the tiny psychiatrist on both cheeks.

"Mort?" Susan said, "Is that what your friends call you? That's French for Death, isn't it? Makes sense as your middle name I guess."

"Don't I know you?" she said to Uriel. "Didn't you helped me get into Medical School when everyone else said I would never have a chance with my grades and my folk's financial status."

"You got it kid. I'm the Archangel of Inspiration and Wisdom. You always had the smarts to make a go of it in medicine. I just had to give you a push and then grease the path for you. I did the same thing for King Solomon, but then he got himself tied up with all those wives and slid into apostasy with all their false Gods."

"Solomon was just another spoiled kid from David's household," said the other new visitor in a rumble deep voice. "I probably could have straighten him out if they had given him to me to run him through my angel boot camp. Lucifer was the only failure I ever had and for the same reason. Too much power, too soon, is terribly addictive."

"Now Michael, that is old news and you can change none of it," said Gabriella sadly, a startling silver-haired Viking princess, she took Michael's right arm and settled next to the chief Archangel and leaned her cheek on his right shoulder. Michael was dark, dressed in a chocolate leather suit, and radiated strength and calm. He and Gabby made a startling combination of contrasting and complimenting features. "Your stew smells delicious as usual, Raphaella, but I think I'll just have a piece of pie. Working through the problems of Earth always tends to upset my stomach. So much evil; so much hatred. Why can't they ever learn to follow the rules and simply obey?"

"Guys, we have to run. I've got to get back to work straitening out the Egyptian mess. We only stopped so Raphaella could clear out Susan's cancer so she can travel with me. We'll stop back in a week or so after I have carried out the Creator's orders on the Passover. Maybe we can see you then." Standing Dr. Samael kissed both of the female Archangels on their cheeks, bumped fists with Michael, took Susan's hand, and stepped somewhere else.

There was sand everywhere and the air was throat-clenching dry.

"What a nice bunch of people, ere angels. They didn't seem to have any problems accepting you and your profession. Maybe your are just being a little paranoid about the job and are projecting your feelings onto those around you," Susan said. "Tell me a little about what you do and how you do it. Do people know you are present when you come to collect their souls? Do they struggle and resist you? I know it must be difficult to give up all they have ever known, even if they are moving on to better things."

"My job is simplicity itself. There is a spot on the back of your neck, it appears to me as a crimson dot, all I have to do is touch it and your soul is released into my hand. I see you as a ghostly projection of yourself. You have a full compliment of arms, legs, hair, fingers, toes, and right in the center is a glowing pearl, bigger in some and shrunken in others, who have done little to increase its size."

"A pearl? I don't remember anything like a pearl in my Anatomy books. What is it and where is it located?" Susan asked.

"Wrong book," said Mort, "You need to look in the Bible, in Genesis. When God created Adam, the first man, he breathed into his nostrils and brought him alive by the breath of God. The Jews call this breath, the Rhuach. God's breath was the seed, the nucleus, for the first Pearl. Every human from then on has within them the Pearl of God. Jeshua, he who was the Word of God, says that you have your very breath and life in him. As you live and serve God, you receive many in-fillings of the Holy Spirit, which layer out on this seed of God.

Many of you leave the body with a pearl of great value from living a life filled with obeying and serving God. Some of you leave with a pearl coated with shame and willfulness that you must take with you as you return to God. God values you all because you have within you a part of Him; you all are seeded with God's essence. God does not give up easily on his seed and will send me even into Hell itself to retrieve it. That is not an enjoyable journey I must assure you."

"As to your question about whether people see me when I come to collect their soul, there is no easy answer. You can see me, so I assume they can all see me. Do they know I am Death? Most people are not very observant. I don't wear a black robe and carry a sickle like many of the illusions of Death demand. I don't scream like the Ban She or have a foul smell like Thoth. I look pretty much like a normal human until I touch their necks. A few people get upset at that point, but its pretty much a done deal. I can't put them back in, you know. I take their hand, step sideway, and we are at their destination, wherever that happens to be. It is always so fast that they are all a little disoriented, so I try and explain what is happening before I leave them to their fate."

"You can't handle the workload of all those deaths in one day and night, can you? How do you ever get done?" Susan asked.

"You are right," said Dr. Samael. "I can't do it all by myself. For the first couple of millennium, things were pretty slow. There was only the occasional accidental death. But after the fall and Satan's interference in the Garden of Eden, things began to pick up. When Adam, Eve, and their children lost their access to the tree of life they began to age. But, they still lived a long time before I had to collect their souls. Things began to speed up when God decreed that the age of man was limited to one hundred and twenty years at the time of the Great Flood. I went to God and complained that I couldn't keep up and tried to resign so he could appoint a more efficient angel. He told me to *bloom where I am planted* and assigned me a whole cadre of death angels to work with me. It was only a temporary position for them. Whole legions of angels were assigned to work with me on a rotating basis. Most of them escaped as soon as they could get reassignment back to their own Archangel. I touch their hand and they gain the releasing power, but lose it when they manage to get a new assignment. I am always short-handed and falling behind. A few of my death angel cadre have stayed with me through the millennia."

"As we get closer to the end of the age, there are more people alive then as any time in history. In fact there are as many people alive today as there have been in all of human history. I have no idea how I am going to be able to collect all of these souls. I can only do what I can, take care of the difficult collections, and hope that God will mobilize the heavenly hosts to help me out at the end."

"It sounds to me like you have an administrative problem," Susan said, "Do you have a list of all the angels who have worked for you any time in the past? When you really get pressed for time in the future, you can use that as a draft list. You can call them up on an emergency basis. They already know the techniques you use. You can run them through Michael's boot camp to get them to move speeded-up again. Where have you taken us? What is this place?" Susan asked.

"Do you remember your Old Testament Bible? We are in Egypt of Ramses II approaching the Exodus of the Hebrew slaves. Moses has sent the first nine plagues to curse the Egyptians. Tomorrow he will send the last plague and force Pharaoh to let his slaves go. I must collect the souls of the entire first born of the Egyptians in one night. Two weeks from now I must collect the souls of Pharaoh's army drowned in the Sea of Reeds. I'm going to be very busy even though I can move at the speed of thought. You must help me hold it together as I take the souls of those innocent children. But, you will need a change of clothing. I think you would look best as a nurse of the nobility. With your permission, I will change you."

In a flash, Dr. Susan was transformed. She was dressed in a white-linen long dress with her left breast free, an ornate belt of gold, and gold snake bracelets pushed up high on her biceps. Her medical bag was transformed to a canvas bag with rope handles. Her shoes were transformed to beautiful gold-trimmed sandals. Looking down at her bare breast, she blushed furiously.

"There! You should fit in on any street in Rhamese. I have had to darken your hair with henna to help you fit in. Here is a Persian shawl, but you'll probably not need it until the sun goes down. Stay close to me and keep your hand on my left arm. If we get separated, trust that I will find you. Are you alright?"

"I'm not sure how I feel about public nudity!" Susan said. "I have always been a little sensitive about my height and body shape. I have never been what you would call over-developed."

"You look lovely. Look around. You fit right in. You make a lovely redhead. Your shawl will cover your shoulders and can be pulled up over your head and face."

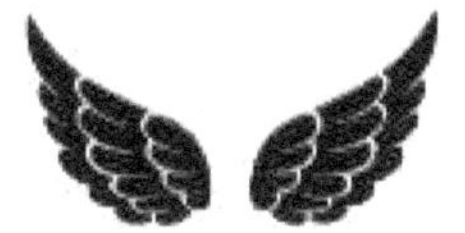

Chapter Two
Egyptian First Born

"I am confused," Susan said. "Your first office call was on last Friday, the thirteenth of September. I was born in 1990, and if I understand correctly, you are saying that we are standing in Egypt in the spring of about 1250 B.C. preparing for the Passover and the death of the entire first born of Egypt. Is that correct? And I can understand the speech of all the people around me. Is that correct? How is all that possible?"

"At the moment I have removed the confusion of your tongue," Matthias said. "All I did was remove the babble of your tongue that Michael placed on mankind at the time of the building of the Tower of Babel. If someone speaks to you or you speak to him or her, they will understand you in their own tongue, be it Egyptian, Ethiopian, Hebrew, or Cretan Greek. Eventually you will be able to understand Koine Greek, Arabic, Roman Latin, and later languages as they come into use."

"But, how can I be here in my own past?" Susan asked.

"It's not your past. As you said, you were not born until 1990. Time in your body is different from time outside the world. Heavenly time is not based on the ticking of your heart or the movement of stars and planets. The best description is in the Bible: *Is, Was, and Shall Be.* Those are places and you can be in any of them, but you cannot change things there. I however can move into the past, present, and future and make changes. My biggest job so far has been going back into the time of Noah and the flood to release the souls of all the unbelievers of his time. I got that one done, learned how to do it, and planned to use the same techniques on this job."

"What is this village? I know we are in the Nile delta, but I don't remember their being mud-dab villages like these between the river and the Sea when I worked a two-year residency in Egypt before I graduated from Med School," Susan asked.

"This is one of the two make-work village that Pharaoh Rhamese created to put the Hebrew people to labor in. The people had grown so fast that they were swamping the land. He had them making sun-dried mud bricks filled with straw. When Moses complained about this brutal labor, Pharaoh doubled their brick quota and made them search for their own straw. It's in the Bible. This town was called Rhamese after the Pharaoh; the other one over there by the coast was called Pithom. With almost a million Hebrew slaves to control, he was forced to find exhausting work for them so they would not revolt. His father had tried to control their population growth by ordering the Egyptian midwives to strangle the newborn Hebrew male babies. That led to the strange story about Moses' birth and recovery by Pharaoh's daughter from the river's water. He was raised as her son, a Prince of Egypt, until he killed an Egyptian overseer of the Hebrew and fled into the desert." answered Matthias.

"How terrible," said Susan, "But, I guess working them was better that just killing them."

"Pharaoh couldn't do that. He needed them to fill the ranks of his army and for his public works projects. His people were building his temples and his burial chambers in the Valley of the Kings. He needs his slaves to cook and clean for them: to make their bread and beer."

"Beer was not a luxury here, the waters of the Nile was filled with parasites that were killed by the alcohol in the beer. The Hebrew slaves also filled the ships that the Cretans built for Egypt. Those Greek survivors of the great tsunami that destroyed their civilization brought technology to the Egyptians: the great ships that hauled giant stone down river and iron tools for weapons and building. Both hated these Philistines Cretans, who occupied an economic level between the Egyptians and the Hebrews. Most of them have already begun to move North up the great Sea coast where they could build their own cities on the coast and where they could build and test their great weapons of mass destruction, the chariots that revolutionized warfare."

"When will you begin this collection of the souls of the first-born?" Susan asked.

"The chosen people must first slaughter their lambs and smear blood on the lintel to protect their own first born. They work hard all day and eat their evening meal after the sunsets. I think it best that you stay here in the kibbutz while I get started in the royal cities on the river. I will work as fast as I can, but I will need a break. I will set loose and transport as many as I can stand before I come to you to seek solace. Fortunately, not all the first-born will be children," Matthias said with a shutter.

In a blink Matthias was gone. Susan heard the sound of a child crying from one of the huts before. She leaned her head through the door way and said, "I am a healer. May I be of assistance?"

The young woman in the only room looked at her in panic. "Oh, my lady, my son is always hungry. He picked something off the floor while I was preparing the blood for the lintel and he tried to swallow it. I think it is stuck in his throat."

"Let me have him," Susan said. Quickly she felt his throat, felt the shape of the object, and tried to move it up toward his mouth. Shc carefully put her finger into the back of his mouth and touched the object. It moved a little but stayed where it was. She reached around the tiny body, grasped her hands under his diaphragm and pulled hard. The child let out a gasp and began to cry. Susan turned him upside down and shook him until an odd shaped rock fell out. The boy reached for the rock and his mother quickly slapped his hand.

"Finish your work on the doorway. Give your child a sop of bread dipped in wine. That should comfort him and ease his pain," Susan said. "Is this boy your only child? The prophet Moses said you must protect him with blood on the door lintel. Where is his father? He may also bc a first-born son. Are there other only children or first born that need protection? The Angel of Death is coming, but will not take the blood-sealed."

"I thought that was only a superstition," said Miriam. "Joash, come inside quickly. Will you stay with my son for a moment? I must get my friend Hechta and her baby, they are first born also. But, she is Egyptian will the blood protect them? She is a good woman none the less."

"I don't know," Susan, answered truthfully, "all we can do is try. Run and get her and we will see what happens."

Miriam returned as her other guests who were to share the evenings roast lamb cooked with bitter herbs began to arrive. She introduced Hechta carrying her child. Then she dipped her hand into the bowl of lamb's blood and placed some on her friend and her son's foreheads and then did the same to herself. "May the God of my people protect you both throughout the evening and into the dawning morning."

Throughout the fading light of evening a wailing sound began to fill the air. Not everyone among the people had believed and protected their family. The families of the Egyptian first-borns among the guards and supervisors began crying as they mourned the loss of their children and mates. Fog rarely seen in the Goshen Delta settled on the land as the people cried out in anguish over their loses. And suddenly, Matthias stood beside Susan. He looked haggard and beaten.

"Are you alright," Susan asked. "You look awful." She forced him to set down, climbed in his lap, and wrapped her arms around him. "Miriam, this is my good friend, Dr. Matthias. He has just come from attending to some of the dying."

"Then there is a plague out there? Is it contagious? What are the symptoms?" Miriam asked.

"No, nothing like that. No wasting, no fever, and no outward sign. Apparently healthy people are dropping dead in the streets. I saw a man fall off the side of a pyramid. He was dead before he hit the ground," Matthias said. "A women was preparing supper and dropped dead over her table. It was terrible because I could do nothing to prevent it. I have just come from the house of Pharaoh. His grown son, his heir, is dead in his bed, as is his favorite granddaughter and his favorite wife. He had surrounded his dwelling with priests and magicians from all nations to protect him. All the first-born among the Egyptians seers and priests are scattered dead around his house. This is a national tragedy of the first order."

"Wait," said Miriam and Hechta at the same time. "Pharaoh's palace is a three days drive in the fastest chariot from the Land of Goshen. How could you know already about the deaths in his family?"

Susan answered, "I only gave you part of my friend's name. His full name is Dr. Matthias Mort Samael. He is the Archangel of Death. The Lord God sent him to Egypt to fulfill Moses' curse. He is here as the protector of the Hebrew, the chosen people. Pharaoh will send soldiers and priests to kill Moses. Instead the assassins will all die. Death will continue to stalk the Land of Egypt until Pharaoh lets the Hebrew people go out of the land. Pharaoh still has to learn this lesson. I wanted to thank you for your hospitality while Matthias was doing his work. I must take him someplace where he can safely get good and drunk. It is not easy being the Angel of Death, but this day has been especially awful for him. Love you all. Be safe."

As Susan finished, she touched Matthias' right arm and they jumped to the lane in front of Raphaella's green colonial house. They knocked on the door. Uriel opened the door and caught Matthias as he fell into his arms. Uriel picked him up and carried him into the guest bedroom on the right. The Archangel of Inspiration tucked Matthias in, and Susan crawled in to cuddle with him as they drifted off to sleep.

Susan was in the kitchen eating breakfast the next morning talking to the Archangel Raphaella about cures for Alzheimer's disease, Duchene Muscular Dystrophy, and many resistant cancers. Matthias staggered into the room and said, "Coffee?" Raphaella pointed to the chair next to Susan and a large cup of steaming coffee appear on the table. “Thank you, my love,” Matthias said as he settled into the chair and seized the cup. “A little touch of whiskey to take the edge off? Good. Thank you. How are you feeling this beautiful day?” He asked the ladies. "Ready for another trip into the desert?"

“Sure,” Susan said. “I thought we were done with Pharaoh.” “People with absolute power are never easy to deal with,” Matthias said. Ramses is over the shock of the death of his son. Now he wants revenge. He sent his assassins to deal with Moses and got dead bodies back as his reward. Now he has sent out his army and his chariots that defeated the Assyrians' forces, to punish, and recover his slaves. The army of slaves has them cornered with no escape against the Sea of Reeds. The Egyptian army is only awaiting Pharaoh’s arrival to press the attack.

“Oh, I remember what the Bible says about this,” Susan said, “God held the Egyptians back with a pillar of fire. Moses called on God holding Aaron's rod in the air and God parted the Sea building it up on both sides so the Hebrew people could cross on dry land of the sea bottom over to the Sinai Peninsula.”

“Very good, my love. That is exactly where we are in time. Behind you is the pillar of fire on the other side of the Hebrew slaves. On the shores of the Reed Sea is Moses and in a moment the Lord will open the waters.”

Moses lifted the staff into the air and with a roar that made Susan's ears ring and pop, the waters began to divide and build up on either side of Moses. Shortly the muddy sea floor appeared and formed a straight path toward the far shore. “Follow me!” Shouted Moses as he climbed down the shore into the drying sea bottom and ran toward the far side. His leaders and Matthias and Susan, charged after him followed by the rest of the people carrying their children and all the riches that had been showered on them by the Egyptian people to end God's curses. As the last Hebrew slave climbed down the shore into the dry sea bottom, the pillar of fire followed them into the sea bottom.

"They are escaping," shouted Pharaoh on the shore. "A basket of gold to the first man who brings me a pair of Hebrew ears." His chariots lined up to rush down the path left by the escaping slaves down to the dry sea bottom. Foot soldiers and dart casters raced after them to be in on the kill. All that stood between them was the pillar of fire advancing toward the Hebrews at high speed. Everyone knew that water would quench fire. For four hours, they raced a crossed the sea bottom until the last Hebrew climbed up on the far shore.

Susan stood next to Moses on the Sinai edge as he dropped his arm holding the staff above his head. The pillar of fire disappeared in a flash. The bottom of the sea turned deep brown and began to stick to the chariot's wheels. Matthias disappeared and the drivers of the leading chariots started falling over dead. Their archers followed them even though some managed to release a few arrows toward the people crowding the shore. And then the walls of water towering over the sunken sea bottom began to slowly collapse. The empty chariots began to jam up and block the way out to the Sinai shore. The Egyptian army tried to turn around and escape back to the Egyptian shore, but their feet sunk into the mud as one after another, they all dropped dead. Finally, the towering walls of water collapse back onto the carnage of the bodies of the army of Egypt. The waters met in a giant pillar of spray, which collapsed as it sprayed both shores. All that was left of the pride of Pharaoh was the dead bodies of his soldiers floating on the water.

Matthias appeared next to Susan and looked out over the bodies floating on the surface and said, "That was much easier than the collection of the new born. Those fellows were all professional killers before they ever arrived here. That, my dear, is why the world calls me Samael, the Venom of God. Come we need a quick vacation before we head to Jerusalem for my next job."

Chapter Three
Death in Jerusalem

"You only got me down here, so you can see my nearly naked body in this string bikini," said Susan to her friend Matthias down on the beach at Ipanema.

"That's not exactly true, but you do have a lovely body and it is tanning up nicely. But, I did have business here with the Jewish refugees that came over by boats during the Diaspora and got caught in that revolution going on up in Cozumel. This area always keeps me busy. The Aztecs and Incas are all blood worshiper and insist on doing virgin and prisoner sacrifices. They have those special holidays where they harvest the beating hearts of their victims to place before their blood-thirsty Gods."

"Where do people come up with ideas like that" Susan asked.

"It's all about power and politics, I guess. It probably seems fine if it's not your beating heart that is torn from your chest," Matthias said.

"I thought you said you have a big job in Jerusalem to take care of. What are we doing hiding here in pre-Columbus South America?"

"Well I thought the beaches would be less crowded now, if you wanted to do full nude sunbathing."

"In your dreams," Susan said. "When are we going back to work on your list?"

"Now, I guess," said the Archangel of Death. "I'm stalling because the Lord wants me to do another mass collection. Do you remember in your Bible in 2 Chronicles when the Assyrian army had Jerusalem under siege in the time of King Hezekiah, and the prophet Isaiah? King Sennacherib of Assyria taunted God by claiming he could not protect them from his army of 175,000 soldiers?"

"Yes, I remember that you had to collect the souls of that whole army when it died in a single night. But, that should not be so bad, the number are only slightly more than the Egyptian army raised against Moses and the people fleeing slavery in the Land of Goshen and the Assyrians are all harden soldiers," said Susan.

"That event itself was not so wearing as the fact that it was only the beginning of the harvest of souls of the Jewish people in and around Jerusalem and out into Israel and Judah. The Assyrian armies were all non-believers who decimated the people of God. I will enter the camp of the unbelievers as dusk falls and let fog sweep over the sleeping men. My work will be over by dawn, but I will have to escort the souls in batches to their resurrection destinations. I will also have to collect the souls dying of starvation in the city: men, women, and most of all children. That will be preparation for my later mass collections during the time of King David and later kings," Matthias said.

"Many will see my actions as the Lord's punishment on the Hebrew people for their disobedience of the laws of the Lord in the covenant that he created for Moses. For instance, the great King David brought punish down upon the people because he ordered a census taken through his land for tax purposes. The Lord God decreed punishment for his transgression and offered David a choice of punishments. In one night, 60,000 people died and I have to collect their souls: men, women, and children, innocent of any fault of their own, and dead because of David's sin."

"How awful!" Susan exclaimed.

"That's only the start," Matthias replied. "David was a general as well as a king. His armies fought everyone in the neighborhood: that meant civilian casualties as well as soldiers throughout his long life. And his family fought each other and tried to seize the throne leading to more deaths. The man had no discipline control over his own children. Eventually, his son Solomon came to the throne and his first job was to kill off all of his siblings! Fortunate he missed one named Nathan, who would be the ever-so-great grandfather of the Virgin Mary. Solomon built the first Temple to worship the Lord God as well as a magnificent palace to worship himself. He filled the palace with his women and children. He told his people to worship the Lord God Almighty and then turned around and built temples so his wives could worship their own gods. God had told the people to have no other gods. Solomon married the neighbor's princesses to expand his territory. But, by doing so he led his people down the slippery road to apostasy. When his sons fought over his kingdom after he died, they attracted the neighbors, who all had grudges against David and Solomon and wanted their property back. Eventually, the worship of false gods lead the God Almighty to take his protective hands off his sinning people and let the Assyrians and Babylonians sweep down, first on Israel in the North, then on Judah and Jerusalem."

"In your times, you talk about the Babylonian Exile without thinking what that meant," Matthias said. "Jerusalem was a city of over two hundred thousand people, the center of worship of the Lord God. It was under siege at least three times. When that happened first the cats and dogs disappear, then the rats were caught, and then the children went into the stew pot, and the people began to call on their neighbors with a knife. The Babylonian only carried about 30,000 people off to be their slaves and they were the lucky remnant. The rest were left for me to collect. Similar things happened in Israel in the north when the Assyrians carried them off in exile and scattered the remnant among their nations."

"This reaping of a nation, even one as small as the Hebrews, created a tremendous workload for me in a very short time. Now I have to go back and clean up the mess. And we haven't even yet gotten to the time of Jesus and the Romans."

"But, why is it so important that you do it now?" Susan asked.

"Because the times grow short and the soul harvest must be completed before the end." Matthias replied.

"What does that mean?" Susan asked. Matthias gestured at Susan and she found herself dressed in Jewish peasant robe and shawl of the turn of the millennium.

"It means what it means. Stay with me, Sweetness, and I'll show you." Dr. Matthias answered.

Matthias started on the fringes of the Assyrian camp as darkness fell and fog began to rise up the Jericho road into the hills and valleys around Jerusalem. He continued by taking the troops guarding the campfires and then flashed through the sleeping men, commanders and the lowliest food soldiers. No sound echoed through the camp except gasps and moans. His work was done long before the sun rose over the Mount of Olives.

"Put your hand on my arm," Matthias said to Susan. "We have a date with King David."

They stepped sideways into a royal bedroom where the great King was praying while a harp played quiet in the corner. "Do not take my people, Dear Lord!" He cried and wept. "Take me in their place. The sin is mine, not theirs!"

Susan let go of Mort's arm to go comfort the king in his pain. The Archangel of Death flashed out of the room and through the palace out into Jerusalem and through the hills surround the city. Cries rose from the city surrounding David's house as people woke to find their love ones dead beside them. The voices of the women of Judah rose in a lament for the dead. David fell to the floor and covered his ears and wept as though his heart would break.

Matthias appeared at Susan's side and simply said, "Come" as he placed her hand on his arm. In a moment they left the King's palace and step forward to a lush valley filled with battling troops and chariots with wheels sunk in mud. "That is the Jezrael Valley!" said Matthias as he left her standing for only a moment and then return. Next, she found herself standing before a striking palace burning at the foot of a mountain surrounded by troops in chariots. "Welcome to Samaria." Said the Archangel as he disappeared to take care of business. Then Matthias was back grasping her hand and they were on a seaside mountain looking down on a city being pillaged, with parts of it on fire. "The Assyrians have put Carmel to the torch!" The survivors will be led out with fishhooks in their noses. They are survivors of the great Punic fleets that once sailed the great Sea as traders and pirates. They go into exile scattered throughout Assyria and Persia and other cities of the empire. "Excuse me for a moment. I have business to attend."

Within a second Matthias was back, taking her hand. "We have one more stop to make in Susa, one of the capitals of Persia in the time of Queen Esther. She has just averted the genocide of the Jews by Haman, a royal advisor to her husband, Ahaserus, the Great King. That is Haman hanging on the gallows he prepared for her Jewish uncle. In a moment, his seven sons will join him. Haman had bribed the king into issuing an irreversible order to have all the Jews in the 27 states of the Persian Empire killed on a given date. Esther has received another order from her husband allowing the Jewish people to defend themselves against their enemies on the day before the genocide day. This will be a blood bath of epic proportion and I must attend to it in a single day. Stay here. You should be safe here in the Royal Persian harem until I return for you."

Susan looked down to find herself dressed in transparent layers of filmy silken pants and bare midriff, a veil of all things, and beaded slippers. This was worse than the string bikini. You could see everything!

In a moment, Matthias was back grasping her hand, "I have to take a break! I have got to deal with the world conquerors next and all the mess they make. Alexander and his armies swept through Persia, Egypt, and the land east into India. Their successors the Roman built great roads, but they couldn't go anywhere without breaking everything around them." Stepping sideways they stood on the path before the green colonial two-story house belonging to the Archangels Raphaella and Uriel.

Susan looked at Matthias and was shocked. His face had a grayish cast to it, there were dark rings under his eyes, and his shoulders slumped like an old man. She tucked herself into his right side and pulled his arm over her shoulder and helped him up the steps onto the veranda. Matthias knocked on the door and waited for Raphaella to open it. The archangel gasped when she saw him and pulled him in.

"What have you done to yourself?" The healing Archangel asked putting both of her hands on his face as she leaned in to him. She took a deep breath and power seemed to fill the room. Matthias' color improved, the rings under his eye and the wrinkles in his face disappeared, and he straightened up and gasped. "Into bed with you right now. I'll fix you something to eat when you get up."

Turning to Susan, Raphaella said, "What has he done to you, my dear? Are you comfortable in that ridiculous costume? You look like a belly dancer. It is not nearly warm enough!" With a flick of her wrist, she dressed Susan in underwear, blue jeans, a blouse, and a

Mickey Mouse sweater. On her feet Susan found the most beautiful pair of brown, butter soft half boots.

"Thank you. Oh, thank you! I have never been so embarrassed in my life," Susan said. "Can I set down for a moment? We have had a busy day. We have travel over a millennium in time throughout the entire near East. I didn't know you could get jet-lagged time-traveling." Susan staggered into the kitchen and slumped into a kitchen chair.

"Oh, my dear." Raphaella said, "We have mistreated you terribly! Males are such beasts some times. Here let me help you." The healing Angel put both hands on either side of Susan's face. In a moment the doctor felt as fresh as spring as Raphaella's wintergreen perfume filled her lungs and a lullaby filled the rooms.

"Oh, my!" Susan said, "That was wonderful. I wish I could learn to do that. My patients would love it. Could you teach me?"

"Why, of course I can. Am I not the Angel of Healing?" Raphaella placed her hand on either side of Dr. Hernandez's face, leaned her forehead on Susan's forehead, and began to hum her lullaby to her. Susan felt warmth and comfort flow in and fill her. "I should have thought about this earlier. It is how I train my disciples among my younger angels. When you need to heal someone touch their face, lean your forehead against their cheek, and hum a lullaby to them. Go try it out on your traveling companion." Raphaella said.

Susan yawned. "I think I will," she said yawning again. She went into Matthias' bedroom, slipped her boots off, and crawled into bed with him. She touched his face with her hand, leaned her forehead on his cheek, and hummed Raphaella's lullaby to him. He rolled over a little and kissed her. Susan cuddled against him and went to sleep.

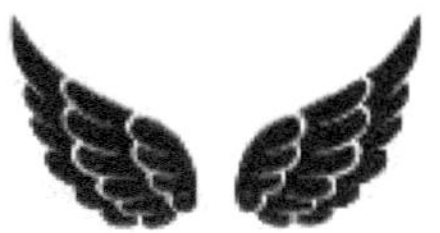

Chapter Four
Punic Wars and Roman Diaspora

Susan awoke in a cooling bed to the smell of cooking bacon. She sat up and pulled on her new boots and staggered into Raphaella's kitchen. Matthias and another beautiful angel were eating breakfast with the Healing Angel. Raphaella said, "Good Morning, my Dear. Are you ready for something to eat?"

"Coffee," said Susan with a yawn, "with milk and sugar. Lots of coffee." Looking at the stranger at the table, she smiled and said, "Hello, I'm Dr. Susan Fernandez."

"Good morning," he said, "another of my healing Angels. My name is Jeshua, although I believe in your day your Bible called me Jesus. Actually, that is the name the Greeks among my followers hung on me. I believe that name came from my mother's nickname for me, Jessy. Of course, she only used that name when she wasn't mad at me. Then, she yelled at me and called me Jeshua Bar Josef. I am so pleased to finally meet you, Susan."

Shocked, Susan gasped, "Jeshua? You're the Messiah? The Son of the Living God?"

"Well yes, but I prefer the Son of Man. You can call me Jes or Jeshua; I'm not much into all that religious formality. I wanted to stop over and meet you before you travel on with Mort into my time on Earth. Seeing the Carpenter from Nazareth in the flesh is always something of a shock for you Christians. I guess it's all those paintings and statues that you display in your museums and churches that gave you the wrong impression. Most of them were done by white Anglo-Saxons, who wanted me to look just like them."

"I want to thank you for your willingness to travel with my Archangel of Death, help him with his assignments, and try and keep him sane. He has a terribly difficult job, with a really demanding schedule, and he has to work with many of the monsters among your people," Jeshua said. "I have to run. I have a busy day, but I want to stop over, meet you, and wish you well on your trip. Love you!" Jesus gave her a kiss on both cheeks and was gone.

Susan sat at the table with a silly smile on her face, sipping at the steaming brew in her cup. Occasionally, she would reach up to touch her face where Jeshua had kissed her. Finally, Matthias reached over and set a platter filled with breakfast in front of her and growled, "Here. Eat! You will need the energy."

Susan blinked at him, picked up her folk, and began to address the eggs and bacon on the plate. "Where are we going next?" She asked still smiling.

"First a history lesson. What do you know about Alexander the Great?"

"He was Greek wasn't he?" Susan replied.

"Macedonian, actually," Matthias replied. "After his father was murdered, he became King of Macedon, which gave him a very well trained hoplite army. He immediately used it to conquer the surrounding seven Greek cities, including the one that murdered his father. Since none of them understood the other's languages, he called on his old tutor, Aristotle, to solve the language problem. Aristotle came up with a military command language and made translations into each city's language. Alexander turned out to be a military genius and used this single language to create a single army with a single military attack concept, the flanking hoplite phalanx. He immediately used it to attack Greece's traditional enemy, Persia. The Persian had very large armies, but very little strategy. They only attacked straight ahead as a mob until the enemy was dead or had surrendered. In three very large battles, Alexander defeated three very large Persian armies, then incorporated them into his army as Aristotle wrote a translation into his Koine Greek language."

"With his new army he defeated Egypt and incorporated their army and chariots with another language translation. He then returned to Persia and attacked east into Northern India until he was overwhelmed by the total size of the Indian subcontinent. He returned to Babylon to rest, got married, and then died after swimming nude in the Euphrates after having conquered most of the known world in about ten years. Koine Greek survived him as his legacy! It became a universal language that let his enemies communicate. Eventually, one of his enemies, the Romans, used it to communicate with all of their conquered countries. In one of those countries, Christianity arose and the Bible containing the teaching of Jeshua was written in Koine Greek."

"Alexander's Empire was divided by four of his generals," Matthias said. "A weak Greek Pharaoh in Egypt led their ally, Rome, into conflict with other leaders of Alexander's Empire after Rome had destroyed their own enemy, Carthage, in North Africa. Rome was expanding in search of food and treasures. The Roman citizen army was based on the mandible legion supported by cavalry and enslaved auxiliary ground troupes. Unlike Alexander, they conquered, then stayed, and occupied their defeated enemies adding them to the Roman Empire. This lasted for about five hundred years in the west and fifteen hundred years in the east before Rome collapsed through politics and, eventually, exhaustion. Their Empire stretched from Britain in the west to Asiatic Greece, Constantinople, and Egypt in the South. Rome maintained this widespread empire by building a network of seven-foot deep well-drained roads and well-protected harbors built with hydraulic cement. Couriers, cavalry, and foot armies used the roads to rapidly travel the empire. Roman ships and triremes knitted the empire together by dominating sea travel making the Mediterranean a Roman bathtub. Rome brought the Peace of Rome to its subjects with its weapons, iron-shod sandals, and Roman law. One of those countries was Israel in the time of Jeshua and it was out of this country that Christianity exploded over Roman roads and harbors speaking Koine Greek to become the official religion of Rome in two hundred years."

"Greek and Roman occupations were not gentle conquests. If a country or city resisted the take over, it was opened to rape and pillage for a specified period of time. Israel was the property of Egyptian Pharaoh Cleopatra after she seized it from King Antiochus of Persia. He had become very unpopular by outlawing traditional Jewish religious worship, banned circumcision, and reading of scripture. Israel rebelled against Antiochus, fought wars to throw the Persians out, and invited the Romans into help them. Israel was conquered by a Roman General named Pompey, who entered the Temple's Holy of Holies, which enraged the High Priest. Israel was given to a wealthy Idumaean Arab, Antipater, for a bribe to the Romans to rule and collect taxes. His son, Herod the hammer, was in charge of taxation; he proved to be a bully and a thief, but Rome couldn't care less as long as they got their taxes. Herod came to rule when Antipater was poisoned. Herod married into the Jewish Royal family, ruled with an iron fist, and eventually went mad and killed his Jewish wife and his oldest sons. Rome took over rule of Jerusalem when Herod's oldest remaining son turned out to be even worse than Herod and the Roman's appointed a Roman proconsul to rule in Jerusalem."

"It was under a Roman proconsul that Jeshua was arrested, accused, and convicted by the Jewish Sanhedrin of blasphemy. The Jews were not permitted to execute Jeshua, so they trumpeted up rebellion charges against him, and sent him to Pilate, to do their dirty work. Pilate sent him to the cross," Matthias said.

"Now I have to go to all these Jews killed by the Persian, Egyptians, and Romans and release their souls. Most of all I have to release Jeshua from his earthly body, so he can be resurrected, teach his followers for forty days, ascend into Heaven, and send his Holy Spirit to his followers at Passover."

"What happened to Jeshua's disciples when he ascended?" Susan asked.

"All of the disciples were eventually killed by either the Jews, the Romans, or by barbarians that they tried to evangelize. James the brother of John was the first murdered. Roman authority had briefly faded in Jerusalem, so James was behead at the order of the high priest. Paul and Peter were seized and crucified in Rome at the order of Caesar. James the brother of Jeshua, who lead the Jerusalem fellowship for 30-years, was stoned on the Temple steps at the order of the Sanhedrin. John the Beloved was assigned to prison as a ninety-year old, released three years later, and then died of natural causes before he got caught up in the first pogrom in Asiatic Greece with his student Polycarp," Matthias said.

"How terrible!" Susan said.

"The Roman power in Israel faded briefly. The various Jewish fractions took turns seizing control of the Holy places and fighting each other. Eventually, the Romans under Titus returned with power, first of all in Galilee, Jeshua's, old home. They crushed the Jewish armies, then went south into Jerusalem and stormed the Temple. They set it on fire while priests were still doing the sacrifices. The Romans tore down the burnt Temple, the walls surrounding the Court of the Gentiles, and then burned the city of Jerusalem. They went into the Dead Sea area, wiped out the Essenes, owners of the Dead Sea Scrolls, on the way, and then stormed Herod's Dead Sea stronghold called Masada forcing a bunch of Jewish Zealots there to commit mass suicide." Matthias said.

"The Jews failed to learn their lessons about annoying the Romans. A new Messiah arose name Jeshua Bar Kochba, or Jesus of the Star. The army he led ambushed and destroyed two Roman legions. Caesar Hadrian order Jeshua captured and crucified. His army was fought and destroyed to the last man. Jerusalem was burned again, razed to the ground, salted to keep anything from growing. Jews were barred from the city on pain of death and the city was renamed Aelia Capitolina, after Hadrian's family name. It kept that name until the Moslems took the city in 627 BC."

"It sounds like a lot of the Jewish people died around the time Jeshua lived." Susan said.

"They all died," Matthias said. "That's the way all life ends. The question is how messy the end is. The conquerors were always famous for messy endings. When Spartacus, a slave gladiator, led a rebellion against the Romans in Italy they crucified all the survivors and left them on the crosses till their bodies rotted off. The bodies lined the highway for twenty miles. Now that was a messy ending."
"When are we going to go take care of the Jews and the Messiah? What am I going to wear this time?" Susan asked.

"I thought you should dress as a Roman matron. No one will bother you. Even the Greek-Persians fear the Romans and would never bother their women. Roman women are very independent. They manage their own property and money as well as their family."

"Romans wear sandals, right? Make sure that nothing happens to my boots when we change. I want them the next time we visit Raphaella."

"Yes, my dear," Matthias said. In a moment she was wearing a long linen dress with a purple fringe, elaborate sandals with heels, and a scarlet shawl. Placing her arm on his arm and they stepped sideways.

They found themselves in a living room where three Persia soldiers were chasing a woman and her children around the room with long knives in their hands.
Mort said in a booming voice, "What is the meaning of this?" The soldiers froze in place as Dr. Matthias walked over to each of them, touched a spot on the back of their necks, gathered their souls, and departed. He was back in a moment. Shuddering he said, "Greeks have no esthetic sense! Their Elysian Fields for their dead have no warmth or joy in them at all."

"That was amazing," Susan said. "What did you do? It look liked you froze time for those Persian, but not for us"

"Exactly. A useful tool when the dying person would resist my touch. I almost always use it with soldiers, especially ones carrying weapons. They had orders to rape and kill this family because the lady had her son circumcised and read to them from the Torah," Matthias said. "God wants her to survive and spread the word of this miraculous intervention."

"But, what about the soldiers? They were certainly not dying before you intervened," Susan asked.

"They were all destined to dying in a battle with Icaria rebels later today in an ambush. I just advanced their departure a little in a good cause. I have a little flexibility in such cases. You will see a lot of that as we collect souls here. In most cases, we will arrive mostly too late to protect a family so you must be prepared for some ugly scenes and ugly deaths. King Antiochus is a fanatic about wiping out these people's worship of Yahweh. In his own time, his sons will attack and kill him with knives in the temple of his own god," Matthias said. "Fortunately, I won't have to gather his soul. Persians have their own death God, Ahriman."

"Where do we go after we handle these persecution souls?" Susan asked.

"The Hasmodeans raised themselves an army in the north and eventually drove the Persians back northeast to their home base. But, then the Jewish King John invited the Romans in to guarantee their peace. That was like inviting a brown bear in to protect your dinner. He just pulls a chair up and cleans the table. Then you can't throw him out of the house without inviting in a more dangerous guest. The Hasmodean kings kept getting involved with more and more dangerous guests until they seated various Persian kings, Anthony and Cleopatra, Pompey the Great at the table, and eventually ended up under the protection of Caesar Augustus, Antipater, and Herod the Great. They couldn't find any more ferocious protector so they had to keep what they had," Matthias said. "Which brings us up to the time of Jeshua."

"In the time of Jesus, the Jews were a conquered people, occupied by Roman armies. They had to scrape together every thing they could to pay the Roman and the Temple taxes. Often they had little left to feed themselves and their family," Matthias said. "They were also a divided people: the Zealots and Icaria wanted to fight and throw the Romans out, the Essenes wanted to ignore the Roman and focus on their worship rituals, the Priests and Scribes struggle for what little earthly power was left in the name of the Lord God. After Herod's death, various groups rose seeking the Jewish throne and power over the High Priest. Periodically, the Romans over-reacted through ignorance, and incensed the Jews leading to violence. When Pontius Pilate, the fifth prefect over Judea and Jerusalem came and began his job, he ordered a Roman standard topped with an eagle placed in the Temple grounds to establish his authority. The Jews were allowed by the Torah to have no image of anything on the earth, sea, or heaven in the holy place and they rebelled against this sacrilege. Fanatics tore down this Roman image and many were killed at this sign of rebellion. It was a violent time and any Jew could walk into a protest or be swept into a persecution by armed soldiers."

"Jeshua was accused by the Jews of being just another rebel. Pilate at first seemed to confuse him with Jesus the Egyptian, who had lead a bunch of rebels. Christians consider his conviction and crucifixion to be an utter miscarriage of justice. To the Romans it was just a misunderstanding and of no great importance.

The Jewish authorities were happy to get rid of this apostate troublemaker: they had been trying to arrest and kill him, and now he was gone. They only worried that his followers might steal his body and claim he had risen from the dead."

"It's not his followers they have to worry about, it's me," a deep voice said. "Who is your pretty little bird, Samael?"

"Abaddon, what are you doing here?" Matthias asked.

"Same thing we were doing on Mt. Nebo in Moab after Moses died. We are trying to collect Jeshua's body so Lucifer can reanimate it to use it as the Anti-Christ. He sent me to release his soul before he dies on that cross. I have a signed permission from the High Priest to remove the body. Lucifer failed to get Moses' body because Prince Michael showed up and defeated my master in angelic combat. But there is no warrior Angel here to stop me this time and you were never able to stand up to me, Mort."

"Matthias, who is this beautiful angel?" Susan said. "You must introduce me. I have heard that fallen angels are great in bed. Are you as good of they say? I heard that your children with mortal women like me are heroes and champions. Want to give it a try, lover?"

"Susan, what are you doing?" Matthias asked in shock.

"Hold him for me, Useless! Let me kiss him."

Matthias grasp the dark angel by the shoulders and pulled him away from Dr. Fernandez. Susan leaned forward, pressed her forehead against Abaddon's cheek, reached up and put her hand on his face, and began to hum the melody she learned from Raphaella.

"What have you done to me, you witch?" screamed Abaddon slapping Susan and pushing her away.

"All I did was heal you, Loser. I figured you were ill if you betrayed God's faith in you to follow Satan in his faithlessness. Look at your skin now, traitor. You are snowy white, cleansed of your sin. Creep back to your master, The Prince of Lies, and see if you can explain your failure to him. You are cleansed and healed, but you are still unforgiven. You are stuck forever guarding the Pit until the end of time. See if Satan is as forgiving as I am."

"You whore!" said Abaddon reaching foreword to rip Susan's throat out as Mort touched the red spot in the back of his neck.

Grasping his soul, Samael disappeared for a moment then reappeared to hold Susan in his arms. "Thank you, my brave girl. I would never have thought to do something like that. Abaddon will be better off in Hell rather than facing Satan's fury and explain that a mere mortal destroyed his mission."

"Let's go find Jeshua," Susan said. "I want to listen to him. I have read his words in all four gospels, but now I have a chance to hear himself."

"Come. They will be in the upper room preparing for the Seder meal on this last night before his arrest and trial. Take my arm and walk with me." Matthias said. In a moment they were in a crowded and stuffy attic space stuffed with crates of vegetables and fruit. A tabletop was spread on some of the boxes and servants were placing loaves of bread, plates, mugs, and trenchers on the table. Men and women were sitting on the floor, leaning on their elbows, next to the table, while servants crowded by and stepped over them to put the roast lamb, fruit, and vegetables on the table as other servants poured wine in some of the cups.

Jeshua was going from person to person washing their feet. He said, "As I have washed your feet, you must be a servant to all you meet. I have told you that I must leave you to go to my father. I will ask him and he will send my Spirit into you to empower you and remind you of all that I taught you." He then offered a prayer as a blessing on the meal as the lamb was carved and plates were past. Susan heard Jesus say over the voices around the table that one of his disciples would betray him. A woman setting next to him leaned over to ask him a question as a man with a scraggly beard leaned over to dip his bread in the wine cup in front of Jeshua. The man rose, leaned over to speak to Jeshua, and then rose and left the room. Susan heard a name, "Judas", and the words, "feed the poor."

"Come," Matthias said. "It's time for us to leave!" Putting Susan's hand on his arm he lead her into the street beyond the house and into a Roman prison were a woman and her family were being tortured to death. "Jeshua is not the only one to be arrested, tried, and convicted tonight. She used Caesar's taxes to feed her family and she was accused by her neighbors to the Romans." Matthias touched the necks of the woman and her children, collected their souls, touched Susan's hand, and led them onto the road before Raphaella's home. "The family is settling in their new home. We need a break. Tomorrow will be traumatic enough as is. We need to rest."

When Raphaella opened the door, Matthias said, "Abaddon's sins have been healed and he is freed of his body. I took him to Hell to hide from Satan. Susan used your healing touch to clean him. I never would have thought to try such a thing! This child is totally fearless."

Susan blushed, "I could see he was ill. I just treated him as a patient. I'm afraid I deceived him before I touched him. I'm still working on treating angels. I hope God will forgive me, but it was the only thing I could think to do to help him."

"Bless you, my child," Raphaella said. "Archangels, even fallen ones, are some of the most powerful of God's creations; they stand before the very face of God. Even other archangels tremble before them. But, you saw a need and addressed it. Great thou are and blessed by God!" The healing Angel leaned over to kiss Susan on the mouth placing her hands on both side of her face. "I give you my protection, for I perceive you are going to need it, for you rush in where angels fear to tread."

"Thank you, my teacher. Could I find a bed? I feel like I am going to collapse," Susan said crumbling into Matthias' arms.

"What is this creature you have brought us?" Raphaella said shaking her head.

"I believe she is an overly passionate female human, who possess the compassion that the Lord saw them capable of showing. She continuously amazes me and terrifies me. May God himself protect her," Matthias said carrying Susan into bed.

In the morning Susan awoke refreshed, she pulled on her boots and jeans and headed toward the smell of coffee, bacon and toast. "Morning," she said to Uriel, Raphaella, and Matthias. "You all look so somber. What's the matter?"

"It's Jesus' day to die on earth and none of us are permitted to help him until he is finished. That means you also. But, you will be needed to comfort his mother if you will. Finish your breakfast so we can go," Matthias said.

Susan ate quickly noticing she was dressed in a patched Galilean dress and sandals again. She gulped her coffee, set the cup down, stood, and placed her hand on Matthias arm. They stepped sideways and they found themselves in a scene of horror. Jeshua and two others hung on crosspieces before them. Jeshua had been beaten and was covered with bruises and old blood. Blood streamed from his hands, feet, and down his face where his beard had been torn out by the handful. Trickles of blood streamed from the crown of thorns jammed into his brow. Around the crosses a small group of women wept and cried out in a loud keening cry of morning. A small woman was in the arms of a man, who had been at the last supper. On the cross, Susan heard Jeshua speak in a gasping whisper, "Today you will be with me in paradise."

Susan went to Mary, the mother of Jeshua, where she was held by John, "Dear woman," Susan said placing her hands on Mary's face and leaning her forehead against her cheek, she began to croon Raphaella's lullaby. Susan said, "He will rise from the dead as he promised. God loves his son and has much for him to do yet. He will rise! Do you believe?"

"I believe, but it is so hard. He is hurting so bad as he pushes himself up so he can breathe. As he hurts, so I hurt. I am all right, but please help the Magdalene. She loves him more."

Susan turned to the beautiful woman sitting on the ground with a veil of red hair over her face. "Mary, I come to bring you comfort if you will let me for I am one of God's healer," Susan said as she sank beside Mary the Magdalene. Susan leaned her forehead against Mary's face and laid her hands on her face humming Raphaella's lullaby. "You must be strong for much yet is expected of you. He will rise from the dead and you must be there to receive him. We shall know you throughout time as the one who kept the faith and received him back. Blessed are you, O comforter of Jeshua's mother."

On the cross Jeshua gasp and slump forward. Dr. Samael disappeared and another figured appeared. He had the appearance of an archangel with a sly foxy face, "Gone is he? Then he won't be needing his body." As he turned to the guard with a document in his hand, Susan said, "There is no place for you here, Prince Lucifer. You have done enough harm."

"Who are you to tell my place, woman? I have business here with these Romans."

"So did Abaddon when he was in the grasp of your attraction. But I did this to him and healed him," saying this Susan leaned her forehead on his cheek and reached for his face humming the lullaby. Satan jerked away and cried out, "That is Raphaella's healing trick! Get away from me."

Just then a carriage roll up next to the soldiers and a roly-poly figure hopped out, "Stop! I come with orders from Prefect Pontius Pilate. The body of the one called Jeshua the Galilean has been released to me."

"Release to you? He can't be dead already. He has only been on the cross for four hours. He should last at least another four hours. We've already got our portion, but his clothing will only bring enough for a single drink, for the four of us. Don't shake that paper at me. I can't read it anyway, but I recognize the Prefect's signature. Who are you if he asks? Let me checking on the criminal. He banged Jeshua's feet with his spear and got no response. Finally he took his spear and jammed it into his side receiving a gush of water followed by blood, "Well, I'll be damned. He is dead! I guess the carcass is yours. A fellow can't be too careful. I had to supervise the crucifixion of a friend of mine one time. He was a centurion from Brindisi. Nice fellow, but he took down one of those Iscari murderers before he was ripe. Fellow died almost immediately after he came down off the cross. But, the law is the law. My friend Cassica insisted on it. So we had to nail him to the cross and hung him back up there. Lasted almost two days, he did. Tough old bird, those centurions."

While the soldier was talking, another older man came out of the carriage carrying a ladder. His slave followed with a hammer and climbed up to Jeshua. Using a block he pulled the nails out of his feet and then hands, he slowly worked the body to the ground where the two older men gently carried it to the carriage wrapped in a shroud. The two of them climbed into the carriage, the slave climbed up into the driver seat, and they drove off.

Beside Susan there was a hiss of anger, “This isn’t the ended of this. You have intervened in my business. I will file a grievance with your Archangel. You will see me again.” Satan turned sideway and he was gone.

“What was Satan doing here? I just passed him on the way back. Boy, was he mad!” Matthias asked.

“He tried to steal Jesus’ body while you were gone,” Susan said. “I tried to use Raphaella's healing trick on him, but he caught me and stopped me. Then Joseph of Arimathea showed up with the permit from Pilate to take the body. He and his friend brought a carriage, a ladder and a hammer and got him down. Satan stormed off muttering threats to file a grievance with my archangel. He sounded just like a union shop steward.”

“You are just too much,” said Matthias. “No fear and no sense!” He wrapped his arms around her and hugged her.

“I am not impressed with power figures. I have had to back down hospital heads and department chairmen where patient's health issues were concerned. Where do we go next?”

“The persecution of the saints is about to start. First, by the Jews and then by the Romans. It starts with Stephen, one of the Greek table stewards appointed by Peter. Saul of Tarsus was there when they stoned Stephen and he went to the High Priest to get permission to hunt down these followers of Jeshua to throw them in prison. Many of them died in prison or in resisting Saul's hit teams.”

"Come," Matthias said, "We need to attend to Stephen." Taking her arm they stepped sideways to arrive at a stoning with people in formal dress robes screaming and shouting, "Kill him. Stone him for apostasy. Kill the heretic."

The older men were pulling off their outer garments and cloaks and laying them in front of a young man. They picked up stones to throw down the hill where Stephen stood with his hands raised toward Heaven saying, "Forgive them Lord. They do not know what they are doing."

Matthias disappeared as the first stone sailed toward Stephen. The rock struck Stephen in the head and he collapsed as other stones followed burying him. "Let him turn those stones to bread to give to those he serves," Saul of Tarsus said from were he sat guarding the robes of his elders.

In a moment, Matthias was back with Susan. Taking her arm, they step sideway on to the road leading to the two-story green colonial house.

"From what I remember from my Bible, Saul was confronted by Jeshua while traveling to Damascus to continue his reign of terror against the Jews of the Way," said Susan. "He was struck blind, then had his vision restored, and became a powerful advocate for the Son of Man?"

"A lovely story," Matthias said. "Saul was a rabbinical student from Tarsus in Asiatic Greece. He was a bit of a fanatic and politically ambitious, and very driven to serve the Lord God. He listened to Stephen's defense of his beliefs before he was stoned and it is possible that he may have listened to Jeshua teach. Whatever happened to him on his way to Damascus, there is no question that he had his religious eyes opened. Once he was enlightened, he became as much a fanatic for Christ as he had been against him. When he converted he began to preach to Jews and the Gentiles, he changed his name to its Gentile version, Paulus. Much of his success seems to have come with God-fearers, who were visiting the synagogues. These were Gentiles, who were attracted to the Jewish God, but did not wanting to be circumcised, because they knew they would never be children of Abraham. Suddenly, here was Paul telling them they could have it all, everything the Jews had. In addition they could have forgiveness of sins without sacrifice, and they would have resurrection from the dead and everlasting life. The Jews listened and most doubted, the God-fearers listened, became excited, and many became believers."

"It was not an easy road that Paul chose! He raised hatred among the believing Jews and doubt among the early Christian leaders. On his firsts trip out of Antioch he was stone by Jewish believers and left for dead. His followers prayed over his body and he was raised, which was amazing. I was there and I can testify that his spirit never left his body. He was often beaten and imprisoned. He was shipwrecked twice. Many of his followers received the same punishment and were killed. These early converts considered themselves Jews, who followed the way of Jeshua. In Antioch, they began to call themselves Christians."

"Persecutions of the Jews and Christians began in the time of Caesar Claudius, who order the Jews driven out of Rome and persecuted throughout the Roman Empire.

It was Caesar Nero who recognizes the Christians as separate from Jews and began the first organized persecution. He blamed the Christians for the burning of Rome and seized them and had them murdered as entertainment in the Coliseum. Nero had given orders to burn out the slums in the slave quarters and the fires got out of hand. The Christians were convenient villains to blame for the arson. My work in releasing the souls of martyrs became overwhelming for the first time," Matthias said. "I had to yell for help from Heaven. The first volunteer angel program was put together, but didn't work very well. I had to learn how to work much faster, but I cannot be in two places at once, or three or four. But, I can stop the advance of time for a few seconds so I can handle three or four souls at a time."

"These attacks on Christians accelerated during the Roman War with the Jews ordered by Caesars Vespasian, Titus, and Domitian when the Temple was destroyed. Christians were neutral observers, but in times of war no one is treated as a neutral. Christians were attacked by both sides and suffered terribly. The second Diaspora of the Jews also began at this time. Where they could, they fled their homeland for safer homes. Alexandria in Egypt became the destination for many intellectual Jews and Christians and eventually had the largest Temple outside Jerusalem.

Persecution continued for another 100 years under various rulers until over 50,000 Christian martyrs perished in various terrible ways under the Romans. The Emperor Constantine realize finally that the growing Christian religion could be an ally to unite his growing Eastern and Western Empire and he made Christianity the official religion of Rome. Persecutions continued but they were not sanctioned by the government," Matthias explained.

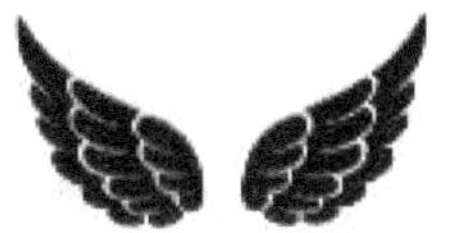

Chapter Five The Huns, Goths, and the Birth of Islam

"Nothing lasts forever," said Matthias said as they sat eating breakfast with Raphaella. "The Roman Empire in the West collapsed for a number of reasons. Bad rulers, drought and famine, military defeats to barbarians in Germany, Spain, and North Africa were the most direct causes. The Visigoth barbarians swept into Germany, France, Spain, and across the Mediterranean Sea into North Africa. Loss of Spain cost Rome its silver and gold mines and loss of Cartage cost it its breadbasket. Eventually the Huns and the Goths swept into Italy and ravaged Rome itself late in the fifth century. Other barbarian groups invading behind them pushed each of these barbarian tribes further into established countries. Most of these were fleeing the push of the Mongol hordes moving into Samarkand, Afghanistan, Persia, and Russia and on toward Europe. The Jews were driven out of Israel by the Roman occupation. They went north into the Russian Steppe and east into Greece, Rome, and Spain, always as a subjugated people pushed into niche jobs, such as money-lenders, political advisors, and doctors."

"The next push on both the Christians and the Jews in Israel was from the south late in the seventh century," Matthias said. "A merchant in Mecca had the habit of taking yearly meditation sabbaticals in mountain caves in the desert. On one of these religious retreats, an Archangel confronted him. Since Muhammad was illiterate, the Angel Jibril had him chant the Qur'an with him three times before sending him home to his wife and family. At home he repeated the Qur'an to his wife, who took him to her uncle, a Jewish scholar in Medina. The uncle proclaimed Muhammad a prophet and recited the holy books of the Torah and the Christian gospels to him."

"In the next twenty years, Muhammad went twice more to chant the Qur'an with the Archangel in the cave in the mountain. Warned that the merchants of Mecca would not receive the chanting of the Qur'an and would drive Muhammad out of town, the merchant chanted the holy book only for his trusted friends. Eventually, he became braver and began chanting the Word of God in the streets and parks of Mecca. He and his friends were persecuted and driven out of town by local merchants, who, were either atheists or clung to their old tribal religions and gods. Some of his friends and believers went to Ethiopia and North Africa to spread the reciting of the Qur'an. Muhammad and his wife went 120 miles north to Medina. There the Jewish merchants attacked his chanting, but he began to collect an army to protect himself. The Word converted an assassin sent from Mecca who eventually led Muhammad's followers quietly back into Mecca. From there they spread north, west, and east into the entire world after Muhammad died. Eventually, the true followers wrote the Qur'an down as drift came into the chanted versions. They also wrote down accounts of Muhammad, his miracles, and teaching in books called the Hadiths."

"Do the Muslim know you?" Susan asked.

"Certainly, for they are also people of the book. They know me as *Malik al-Maut,* the Angel of Death, and some give me the name Azrael or *Help from God*, although that name is not in the Qur'an. At the time of their death as known to the creator, I release their soul and guide them to paradise. They call themselves the People of Peace and they have taken a violent tribal people in what we now call Saudi Arabia and turned them into people ruled by religion and law."

"Muslims are People of Peace? They killed over three thousand people in the twin towers and the Pentagon on 9/11 when Muslims crashed three stolen passenger aircraft into the buildings. They have fought in two wars and killed people at random with car bombs and bombs strapped to martyrs. These are people of peace?"

"These so called martyrs have been misled by the Whabbist fanatics, who preach violence. Muslims are told in the Qur'an that they may only attack to protect themselves and must stop when the attack stops. The peoples killed in the twin towers included one thousand Muslims. Muslim killing Muslims is an abomination as are the other atrocities of that day that will be judged in the last day," Matthias explained. "I will have to release the souls of all of them in a future trip; passengers on the planes, the Whabbist martyrs, and the victims in all three buildings, including firemen and policemen rushing up the stairways trying to save those in the building. I also must collect souls of soldiers blown apart in the desert as well as innocent by-standers killed walking down the street, in a restaurant, or in a mall when attacked by suicide bombers."

"First, we have to deal with the victims of the Diaspora. In the beginning, it was Jews persecuting what they consider blasphemers. Next it was Romans killing rebels among their conquered peoples to protect the Peace of Rome. Once the orders came out condemning Jews and Christians, it was neighbors killing neighbors." Matthias said. "Around the year 500, the growing government of Jeshua's church began to blame the Jews for Jeshua's death and anti-Semitism raised its ugly head for 1500-years of persecution ending in the Holocaust. Also as the church's powers grew so did its attack on heresies: these were Christians attacking other Christians sanctioned by the Church itself. The Holy Inquisition was instituted to purify the church by torturing Christians, Jews, and Muslims into confessing their sins and then killing them while their souls were in a state of purity. The Protestant Reformation grew out of one monk's attempt to change the church's sale of indulgencies or bills of forgiveness of sins.

This led to fragmentation of the Church and eventually to the 30-years War between the Catholic Church and the breakaway Protestant cities and countries. Speculations are that the Holy Church killed more Christians during this war than Rome ever martyred in its whole history. The country of Bavaria, which was eighty percent Protestant at the start of the war, ended up being only ten percent Protestant by the end because of all these religious murders."

"What caused this thousand year orgy of murder?" Susan asked.

"The change seems to have begun around the end of the fourth century," Matthias answered. "Satan had been persecuting the Church from outside for three hundred years and the church had its fastest growth. When Caesar Constantine made Christianity the state religion of the Roman Empire, everything changed. The Church gained power, corruption increased within the church, and the Holy Inquisition appeared to root out heresy. It almost seemed like Satan stop attacking the church from outside, put on church robes, and buried himself inside the Church to destroy it. Church growth slowed and it hunkered within itself during the monastic period. It took the Black Death plagues to shake it out of its hibernation and bring it back to life."

"So how do you handle a thousand years of murder throughout the world? Are they concentrated like the death of the innocents?" Susan asked.

"No, that is exactly the problem," Matthias replied. "The scattered murders I have already handled. It is the concentrated deaths like sieges of cities, major battlefields, and pogroms against concentration of Jews that are a problem.

"Where do you propose to start?" Susan asked.

"When you finish your toast, we will begin with the first round of persecution of the Sephardic Jews in Southern Spain," Matthias answered. “Islamic armies began an explosive expansion in the seventh and eight century up to Jerusalem and a crossed Northern Africa and up into Christian Spain. Like any conquering army they raped and destroyed civilizations in their way, but once they stopped their advances, they brought law and tolerance. Jerusalem was declared the third Holy City to Muslims and was opened to Muslims, Christians, and Jews. For the first time in four hundred years, the Jews could say *Next Year in Jerusalem* and mean it. Jerusalem was an open city of three religions. Islam battled up a crossed Spain and was stopped by Charlemagne’s armies just south of the Pyrenees. They settled in and built beauty in the east central Empire of the Caliphate and in Northern Africa, which they opened to artistic, scientific, and legal growth. Here they maintained the literature and art of Islam, Persia, Greece, and Roman. It spread from Islamic Spain into the monastic communities of Ireland while the rest of Europe slumped into the ignorance of the Dark Ages. Sephardic Jews fleeing anti-Semiticism in the west found refuge in the intellectual tolerance of Islamic Spain. Islam brought with in algebra, Arabic numbers, the concept of zero in mathematical calculations, and a rational observational astronomy.”

Susan found herself dressed in a Roman linen gown bound with a belt holding a very sharp knife in a scabbard, shoulder shawl, and sandals. To this was added a cream-colored tightly knitted facial veil and a headscarf bound round with a gold chain studded with tiny precious gems.

Her arms were bare but on her wrists were bracelets of gold alternating with bracelets made of elephant-hair bound with gold bands. Mort held out his arm, Susan placed her hand on it, and they stepped sideways.

“We are in Valencia in the Caliphate of Cordoba which I will use as my base of operation. You are dressed as a doctor of medicine, one of the few respected professions open to a woman. I would have put you in a burqa, the all-covering garment you see around us, but they are suffocating in this heat. The bag in your left hand contains containers of the herbs and spices used in your profession. I have given you knowledge of how they work their healing. Be careful, they make you a target for thieves, which is why you have a knife on your belt. If you must draw the knife do so cross body and aim for fingers and their crotch, both edges and the point are very sharp if you need to use it. The scar on your forehead and down on your nose is to make you look dangerous and a warning to thieves. You must cover your face at all times, failing to do so labels you as a prostitute in Arabic cultures."

"The large gentleman standing behind you is Josef, one of my angels" Matthias said. "He is disguised as an Ethiopian eunuch, your bodyguard. This is his first field assignment and, if necessary, he can release souls for you if I am gone. We have arrived in a time of intolerance and persecution. The second and third Caliphs were intolerant evangelists and believed in conversion by the sword. The Sephardic Jews and Christians were immediate targets for his beliefs. Caliph Omar Hussein was very creative in the tortures he ordered his inquisitors to use to convert the heretic. I have a number of families to tend to. The Caliph believes in equality of the sexes in his conversion techniques. By the way, one of the greatest sins in Islam is to convert to Islam, even under great pain, and then to recant. Omar knows that the mother of a family is the heart of its religious beliefs, so he goes to great measures to convert the lady of a heretical household. I must go into the ruler's prisons to save his victims while I still can. Be careful. I shall return."

Susan stood in the grass of a park wondering where to start, when a lady in a burqa bowed before her, "Lady, by your garment I know you are an infidel healer. Will you come and heal my children. Our healers can do nothing for them."

"Of course, I will come. What are the signs of their sickness? How long have they been sick?" Susan asked as she followed the woman dressed in black.

"They have the fever. They have a hacking cough, my daughter and both of my sons. It started yesterday and I took them to one of our doctors. He prayed for them and for me. This morning I heard that the doctor died of the same signs and he has black circle marks on his chest and his private part. I am so afraid," said Donna Maria. "My husband was a Register of Cargo at the port, but he did not come home yesterday from work. I sent one of our servants to ask for him and he returned telling me that my husband is dead. Now the servant has the fever and is coughing."

"Take me quickly to your children. Take this handful of herbs, set them on fire in a dish, and carry them throughout the house to drive out the fleas. Get your servants to help you or they to will get the fever and die," Susan pushed the woman into the house. "Get your burqa off and blow the smoke into the cloth of the garment." Susan picked up the oldest child, placed her hand on either side of her face, leaned her forehead, and began to sing Raphaella's lullaby to her. She quickly repeated the same thing to the other two children. "Take me to your servant, who went to the port." When they went to his room they found him ashen and dead still on his bed, black marks were on his face and body. Turning to Joseph, Susan said, "Pick him and his bed up, take it outside and burn everything including these leaves."

Returning to Dona Maria, Susan said, "This disease is the Venetian fever. It is a disease that grew out of a swamp in the Far East. I have seen it before in Athens where I learned my craft. It comes from fleas that live on ship's rats. Burning emphicanthus leaves will kill the fleas. You must tell your neighbors so they can tell the people at the port. Have them carry the burning leaves throughout the offices and throughout the foreign ships. Anyone who dies from the disease must be burned with all his or her clothing and bedding. Bring the ones still alive to me to see if I can heal them. If the disease gets loose on shore, it will turn into a plague that will go from house to house." Donna Maria's children recovered fast and demanded food. Soon their friend's mothers arrived demanding help with their children's fever. Susan went from house to house with her leaves and her healing touch.

As dusk arrived Susan finished her work, returned to Donna Maria's house, and dropped exhausted into a chair. Suddenly there came a banging on the door. When Donna Maria opened the door, palace guards in uniforms pushed their way in. "We have come for the witch!" they shouted. Grabbing Susan they drug her out of the house and up the hill to the Palace.

"Who are you witch and why are you disturbing my caliphate?" asked Caliph Omar from his throne.

"I am not a witch. I am a doctor; a healer trained in Athens, and a crossed the great sea. I was needed to heal children who had caught the Venetian Plague and to keep it from spreading to the neighbors. It seems that it has spread to the Palace before I did." The Caliph was coughing; his eyes were watering as he sat on his throne.

"What are these rumors you are spreading about our trading partners, who bring us the riches of the east, gold and spices? Your witchcraft is probably responsible for that which you blame our friends, the Venetians. People, my Islamic servants, tell me you are going into houses where people are suffering and dying and setting people on fire. Are you a Muslim, witch? No one does healing here, who does not believe in the will of Allah."

"Is it the will of Allah, your Majesty, that you have the hacking cough, the burning fever, and the black circles on your body of the Venetian plague? So be it, I leave you to the care of your Merciful, All-powerful God."

"Stop her! Kill her," Omar shouted rising to his feet, he tottered toward Dr. Hernandez and fell at the foot of his throne. Susan leaned down and felt for a pulse. The court doctors rushed forward. Susan saw Josef reach down and touch the Caliph's neck.

"He is gone," Susan said. "Handle him with gloves. You must burn him with the clothing he is wearing and his bed clothing. Bring me anyone he may have breathed on. Burn these leaves throughout his rooms in the palace. I need to examine his wives and children for signs of the disease." She was taken to the royal quarters, met Omar's family, found his oldest child, a boy, who showed signs of the disease, and healed him as Raphaella had shown her. The only other victim was the Caliph's first servant, who refused to allow the witch to touch him. His rooms were treated with burning leaves until he died in pain and was released by Mort. He was carried out to the pyre where his master was being burned and added with his bed clothing.

After Susan had treated all of his family and received the thanks and kisses of the Royal wives, she collapsed in front of Matthias and had to be carried in his arms to the green two-story colonial house on the path in Heaven. Raphaella met them at the door with a kiss, a forehead on her forehead, and a new lullaby. Matthias carried her into the guest bedroom and tucked her in.

"What happened?" Raphaella asked.

I went to release victims of the first great outbreak of the Black Plague in Spain. I left Dr. Hernandez where she was safe. She found a mother with children suffering from plague, healed them, used your leaves to clean the house, had the other victims and their bedding burned. She used burning leaves to disinfect the source of infection. Then she was arrested by the Caliph, stood by while he raged, threatened her, and collapsed dead of the plague at the foot of his throne. She then calmly healed his heir, the next Caliph, went through the Royal quarters disinfecting it, and when she and I finished with the victims she collapsed and I brought her to you.

"Good you did," Raphaella said. "She had contracted the disease and it was starting to work on her. I healed her and now she will be protected from it. What a wonderful child she is! To go head to head with that monster of a disease with nothing to protect her if she contacted it. Our child is a faithful healer, totally selfless. Truly one of God's own servants."

Chapter Six
Crusades, Black Plagues, and 30-Years War

"How are you feeling?" asked Matthias. "You've been asleep for two days. Raphaella said that I just got you here in time. You caught the plague, but she was able to heal you. You should be protected the next time we run into it. Come, you need to get up, eat, and get some coffee in you."

"Coffee? It sounds wonderful, but I'm going to need a belt. If I stand up without something around my waist, my pants will fall off. I feel like I'm nothing but skin and bones. I'm afraid I need a vacation. Where are we going next and when?"

"I've got some business to take care of in Jerusalem, Constantinople, and Asiatic Greece. Have you ever visited Jerusalem? It's crowded, smelly, but beautiful in its own way." Matthias said lifting Susan out of bed.

As she promised her jeans hit the floor before she could grab a belt loop. Matthias sat her on the edge of the bed so he could summon her a belt. In a moment she had in her hands a belt of smooth links of gold that fasten with a buckle of gold with a sunrise etched on its face. Susan slid the belt through the belt loops and then fastened the buckle, and snagged it tight. "Thank you. Would you steady me?"

She pulled herself to her feet only to be swept up in Matthias' arms. He carried her into the kitchen, deposited her in her chair, then bent down and slipped her socks and boots on her feet. "Eat!" He said pointing at the full plate in front of her.

"Jerusalem," Susan said as she tackled her breakfast like someone would snatch it from her. "What era? It probably is after the Roman desolation, isn't it? Is it after Suleiman restored the city wall? Will we be able to visit the Western Wailing Wall?"

"You sound like one of the *Next Year in Jerusalem* tourists. Usually they are little old Jewish ladies from New Jersey," Matthias said with a smile.

"It isn't my fault. It was my grandmother, Nanna Maria, who was fascinated by the Holy Land. She always wanted to go to Israel to see all the places she read about in the Bible, but she was too afraid of the Arab terrorists to go out and buy a tour ticket," Susan said. "But she spent my childhood filling my head about the Holy City and the Promised Land and all the places I need to see."

"I'm afraid that the Jerusalem we will visit is a different place," Matthias said. "The walls around the old city have been rebuilt, the Al-Aqsa Mosque and the Dome of the Rock have been built, but it lacks its gold dome. It is definitely a Moslem city, the third holiest city of Islam, but it is ruled by a Christian as the Kingdom of Jerusalem. The Knights of the Temple are digging in the basement looking for Solomon's treasures and, when they find them, they won't recognize them at first. Only when they are fleeing Jerusalem following the Templars' defeat at the Horns of Hattin battle will they realize they had found the Holy Grail. They left with Mary's wedding cup and the perfectly preserved copy of the Torah in Moses' hand. They will carry these treasures into Acre on the coast of Outremer and eventually into Southern France. There they will collect them along with Jeshua's Shroud and the Roman Spear of Truth that was said to have pierced his side. The Templars worshiped Mary, the Magdalene, who they called Jesus' most faithful servant and disciple."

"Wasn't she the one that the Pope called a whore, possessed by seven demons, who were cast out by Jesus?" Susan asked.

"Both the Temple and the Church of Jesus have always had major problems with women in leadership positions even though women have always led. Moses' sister, Miriam, and Deborah the

Prophetess lead the early Jews while Pricilla, Lydia, and Timothy's mother and grandmother supported the church in Greece," Matthias said. "According to the *Gospel of Mary Magdalene,* Peter was jealous of Mary's influence over Jeshua and it continued into most of the Popes who occupied his chair."

"Sounds like men in power in my time," Susan said with a grin. Looking down she saw herself dressed again in a Roman gown and shawl wearing her braided gold sandals. "Where are we going?" putting her hand on Matthias' arm.

"We are all ready here," was Matthias' answer. "This was Jeshua's favorite spot to rest and recover when he was in the city. This is the Garden of Gethsemane at the base of the Mount of Olives. He often came here when he needed to meditate and regain his strength. Sit here and let the stillness fill you while I tend to business in the city."

It was so peaceful in the garden that Susan fell asleep, only to wake to a growing roar from across the Kidron valley at her feet. Knights on massive horses rode down the valley followed by an army dressed in blue, red, and grey. They charged up the wide steps before the city walls and battered down the gates under the doubled arched entrance through the city walls. Arabic soldiers who drove them back down the stairs met them. Around to the northern side of the wall other troops scaled crude ladders to attack defenders of the wall just to the east of the Roman Antonia fortress.

In less than an hour, the battle was over. Arabs riding on small ponies rode into the city beyond the Old City walls.

Suddenly, Matthias was back with her. "My work here is nearly done. I just wanted to check that you were all right. Arabic soldiers generally do not bother non-combatants. Here, I brought you your veil and headdress. He changed her back into the costume she wore in Córdoba. "I must go and claim the victims of the Battle of the Horn of Hattin, both Knights Templar, and Arabic soldiers.

The power of the Templars has been broken forever by Saladin, but not without a tremendous cost. The Knights Templar will not surrender and they are being slaughtered. You do not need to see their bloody end. The Kingdom of Jerusalem is no more! There will be other crusades, but the Christians have reached their high water mark. Jerusalem will not be a Christian city again until the Twentieth Century."

"I will come with you. If there has been fighting, they will need a doctor." Susan reached out her hand and they were on a battlefield among the dead and dying. Susan immediately began to triage the wounded, both Arabic and European. The Arabs accepted her treatment, most of the crusaders snarled, struck out at her, and called her a witch and refused her help. A boy with a terrible wound to his stomach cried and begged for help. Susan took his face in her hands, leaned her head on his, and hummed a lullaby. His stomach wound healed as she watched it and the boy climbed to his feet.

"Blessed are you among women," the boy said. "If I survive this disaster, I will make a pilgrimage to Lourdes and become a Jester celebrating the Lord. Thank you, milady, for your miracle of love."

A hand grasp her shoulder and a man spoke in Arabic, "Come with me Holy One. I most take you to my master, Salah al Din." They walked through the battlefield as Susan continued to heal those on the ground, first a wounded Arab, then an English archer, and then a Knight Hospitaller. Eventually, they arrived in a white tent pitched on the edge of the battlefield. Her guide knelt with his head on the ground before the man wearing a turban and a blood-splatter robe. Beside him a curved bloody scimitar was driven into the ground.

"Who are you?" asked Saladin. "I hear you are a healer of miraculous power."

"I am Dr. Susan Fernandez, a healer and companion to Azrael, the Malik al-Maut. I come to heal all who I can and to bring you a warning for your doctors. A great disease curse is coming out of the East for the peoples of the world. Your doctors can help blunt its attack, but not stop it."

"Why do you bring this warning? Are you a believer in Allah or an angel like your friend Azrael?"

"I am a doctor trained in the west. I travel with my friend, whom you call Azrael, to heal and keep him sane. While I go with him, I reach out to heal those I can." Susan answered.

"For what reward?" asked Salah al Din?

"I seek no reward accept the reward of being of use to those who need me. Everyone will die, but I have my reward in removing their pain and prevent some of their suffering."

"Indeed you are a great soul! Let me summon my doctors of medicine."

"Susan," Matthias said appearing on the scene and bowing to the Caliph. "Are you alright?"

"I am fine," Susan said. "I have asked Saladin to call a medical conference with his doctors. I want to offer them a way of protecting themselves from the Black Plague. I just remembered a song, Scarborough Fair, from Renaissance fairs and realized what it meant. It is the ingredients for Four-Thief's Oil to protect those who work with the victims."

It took a while to gather Saladin's doctors, who were treating battle victims. The Caliph ordered them to listen to the Djinn who had come to offer them healing advice. Susan told them of the killing disease that would come out of the East and North.

"It will cause fever and coughing. The patients will show black rings under their fingernails, then boils on their thighs and private parts, and finally black circles on their face, arms, chest, and body before dying in great pain after 7-10 days. Fleas on ship's rats and other vermin carry the disease. Drive the fleas out by burning wormwood and emphicanthus leaves throughout the house. Protect yourselves as you rid the house of the dead with Four-Thief's Oil, made with camphor, garlic, sage, rosemary, lavender, and thyme ground in wine vinegar rubbed all over your body and face.Burn the dead immediately in their bedding, for washing the bedding will not remove the infection. If you wear gloves, burn the gloves when you are through. Cleanliness is next to godliness. You must clean the houses, get rid of the rats, and most of all kill the fleas by burning wormwood throughout the house. Only this will save your people when the Black Death is stalking your homes. Burying the dead will only allow the infection to rise again out of the graveyard."

"Where did you learn all of the this?" Matthias and the Arabic doctors asked.

"Some I learned from you, some from medical school and reading Wikipedia, and some of it from a misspent life at fairs. There is a song that goes *Rosemary, sage, lavender, and thyme, a gift for a true love of mine.* I realize that it was used to make 4-thief's oil in wine vinegar that allowed four French thieves to safely steal from the houses of plague victims." Susan said. "My professor's told us all this while they were telling us the correct antibiotic and vaccines to use to treat plague victims."

"None of which you have at your disposal here in the Kingdom of Jerusalem." Mort said.

"They don't need it now. The plague years won't start here for another two hundred years. Hopefully the traditions and word of my treatment will spread. At its worse, the plague killed 40-60% of the population of the world in the 14th through the 17th century," Susan said.

"How well I know that! Those will be my busiest times," Matthias said. "So far I have flinched away from dealing with these deaths. How am I supposed to range through a dying world to free all those dying victims?"

"I guess you start one step at a time, recruit as many angels as you can, teach them how to move as fast as you do, and then trust the Lord to provide. I learned to get started and run as fast as I could and recruiting help where I could. It worked for me when I was a broke student in medical school. Start with Raphaella, Michael, and Uriel and get them to help you recruit." Susan said.

Matthias was lucky. Plague ships moved in a pattern from East to West, as does the disease. Susan and Matthias started in Constantinople bringing with them Susan's information on four-thief's oil, rats and fleas, burning leaves, and disposal of the dead. With Susan's hand on his arm, they step onto the y-shaped great road in Constantinople called the Mese and went south along the Thief's Way toward Santa Sophia, the greatest cathedral in the Christian world.

They pressed forward toward the Hippodrome, where chariot races were being run between teams of the Blues and Greens. While they watched a team of Greens crashed their chariot into two Blues chariots, which scattered parts and drivers a crossed the sand. Crewmembers jumped over the curbs and fistfights broke out until someone pulled a knife and a full battle ignited. An arrow slashed in from the audience and a riot broke out among the Blue and Green sections of the Hippodrome. An Orator rose from the Emperor's platform and screamed the Riot Act. Soldiers pored down the stairs and up from the entertainer's pits. Swords and spears slashed into the rioters and quickly stopped the fighting. Bodies were drug down the stairs and hauled off into the pits as the race restarted around the chariot wreck, just a normal day at the Hippodrome. A Blue's chariot crossed the finish line first by a nose with foam spraying from the winning horse's mouth. The winners in the audience raced to cash in their winning tickets while the losers in the crowd screamed at and booed the losing chariots.

The next event scheduled was bear baiting by elkhounds, which Susan had no interest in watching. She put her hand on Matthias' arm and they stepped to the Lyceum of the Physicians. A doctor was on the stage talking about the diseases that were being brought into the great crossroad city by the crusaders. "They come from France and England on Venetian ships bringing the pox and scabs on their privates. They come from the East with waterborne disease from drinking from contaminated ship barrels and malaria.

They stop here to beg for money to support their army's and contaminate our cesspools and water sources. What benefit does Constantinople gain from these crusaders? The Emperor must repel this curse of locust and deny them access to our resources before they eat us out of house and home."

"My name is Dr. Susan Fernandez and I come to bring you warnings from east and west. From the Caliphate of Córdoba I bring a warning of invasion. Armies are being raised to bring a crusade against Constantinople. Venice has taken money to provide ships to transport the troops. I have come with God's Angel of Death to bring you a warning of a great killing disease coming out of the East and ways to protection yourself and your patients. I have fought and survived an infection of this disease, which killed the Caliph, ruler of Islam in Spain." She described the symptoms of the Mongol disease, it's normal course, how to dispose of the bodies, how to protect themselves with four-thief's oil and how to make it, and kill rat fleas that cause the disease and how to disinfect building where the disease has been present.

"How do we know that all of this is true?" said the doctor who spoke last. "The Venetian's are our friends. They carry our cargos of spices and silk west and bring us gold and silver from the Franks. We are a nation of merchants. What do you expect to get from this warning? No one does something for nothing! Show us this disease that you warn us about. Surely this is some trick from the Genoese's fleet to cast blame on Venice. We will not get involved in their political struggles to gain more of our shipping."

"Come, Susan," Matthias said. "You have done all you can do here. You have warned them. They will have to debate what you have told them, perhaps a few will write it down and remember when the curse arrives. No one in this city will believe anything they are given for no charge. They do not believe in altruism, anything of value must be sold for a price. Even the Emperor is a merchant at heart. The arrival of the Fourth Crusade will come as a terrible shock to them. The people of the city are Christians. They cannot conceive that the Pope's army will turn on them to seize their wealth. Crusades are supposed to be declared against the infidels, not against other

Christians. They cannot believe that the Pope will consider the Greek Orthodox Church to be infidels who block their access to Outremer and the Holy City of Christ. Christians fighting Christians is as much an abomination as Muslims fighting Muslims in your time. It will be justified for the first time on religious differences rather than an excuse to seize riches to fight a holy war."

"Two places I want you to see before we get on with my work: Ephesus and Corinth. They were two great Roman ports in the time of Jeshua and Paul. They were also two center in the worship of female Greek goddesses: Artemis in Ephesus and Aphrodite in Corinth. They left major temples behind as reminders of their existence. The silver merchant of Ephesus, who made and sold silver representatives of her Temple, accused Paul of trying to destroy Artemis worship. Corinth and its Temple of the Love Goddess on the hill overlooking the city and the port was a major center of prostitution servicing the sailors sailing the Mediterranean. They became major centers of Paul's evangelism, each with problems that required many of his letters of counsel."

Susan had a chance that morning to walk through the remains of the pillars of Artemis's Temple inland from the port of Ephesus. Next, Matthias transported her to the busy port of Chencharea and they walked the remains of the Temple of Aphrodite destroyed by an earthquake on a flattop hill overlooking the city of Corinth and the Roman-built roller canal crossing the Isthmus of Corinth.

Our next stop is the persecution of the Cathars in southern France. They are the first group of Christian heretics being persecuted by the Holy Inquisition. The Cathars were dualists believing in a good God of the New Testament and a bad God, Satan. They rejected marriage, believed in an Earthly baptism to free them forever of sin, and believed that Mary Magdalene was a saint, who greatly helped the spread of Christianity as a teacher. The Pope declared their beliefs heresy and convened an Inquisition to arrest, take them to trial, and execute them if they failed to recant. I must free their souls and take them to their reward. This is just the first such persecution by the Holy Order and the executions will get much more violent against the Jews and Moors in Spain and Portugal. The Inquisition will get worse in

Europe during the Thirty-years War between the Protestant and Catholic Churches.

"At the same time, the Black Plague will surge out of China and the Byzantine Empire in 1355, into Venice and Genoa by sea and spread into southern France, into Spain, on to England, the Netherland, into Germany and Scandinavia, and finally into Russia and Poland," said Matthias. "I will have to deal with victims of both the Church and the plague at the same time. The plague will eventually kill over forty percent of the world's population and continue into the seventeen-century. I have no idea how to begin to deal with that many deaths all at once."

"Recruit other angel, train them to handle the heretical victims," Susan said. "Focus on following the plague as it spreads westward and north. Stay ahead of it with information on fleas, rats, four-thief's oil, and burning victim's bodies and bedding. You handle victims at the epicenter of the infection at your best speed and let newly trained angels pick up the ones you miss. The plague will probably burn itself out as victims and rats die off and survivors show their immunity. Use burning wormwood and emphicanthus leaves to kill the fleas. Teach public hygiene techniques to prevent re-emergence. Use typical CDC methods for treating Ebola infections. Try recruiting newly resurrected CDC saints," Susan suggested. "Typical epidemiology 101 technology. Ask Uriel for ideas and people we can recruit in an all out assault. Make sure that volunteers and recruits have been treated by Raphaella and her trainee Angels so they are resistant to plague and Ebola. Get lists of names of your workers; you are going to need them again when we have to deal with Holocaust victims, Tribulation saints, and in the last judgment."

"Susan, that's brilliant! Let me write that down. You have given me a way of doing this job that I thought was impossible." Matthias said in amazement.

"No," Susan said, That's just taking a typical Harvard Medical approach to a difficult problem. Let's go recruit some Angels and Saints to help us get started and then train them to find other volunteers. *"Each one reach one: each one teach one."*

They left Corinth to walk again on the path leading to the green and white Colonial house. Inside a collection of angels and Archangels were gathered around Raphaella's dining table. Matthias introduced Susan to the gathered host. The subject under discussion was the Black Plague, Ebola, and weaponized plague war weapons.

Susan began, "Mankind is under attack, possibly by his own stupidity. If these problems are not dealt with promptly, man may not survive. Even if we can help control these attacks, Matthias needs help in recovering God's Rhuach seed from the multitude of victims. Saints who worked with contagious disease when they were alive can guide us how these diseases arise, how they spread, how they may be combated, and how populations may be protected from them. But only Angels have the ability to release souls from infected victims and escort them to their destinations. Only the legions of heavenly hosts can move fast enough to release the dying from their bodies and transport them into paradise. And this angelic host must undergo rigorous training to be able to help Samael finish his work before the white throne judgment. This is not his problem alone. This is a heavenly problem. The very will of God is being challenged here. For the Archangels tell me that God's plan does not end this way with a worldwide desolation by infectious disease. This is interference; the Creator has not ordered this. Matthias needs your help."

"Who are you to ask this of us?" Came a voice from the back of the room. "You do not have the aspect of an angel. You look like a human. Let Mort the carrion collector speak for himself and beg for our help. This is no business of yours!"

"Of course, this is my business, Satan!" answered Susan. "These are my people who are being attacked by this curse with which you are saddling mankind. I suspected that you might show up here this afternoon, Satan. I can smell your foul stench behind this invasion and in this room."

"Me? Whenever your kind does something heinous, you try and blame it on me. *The Devil made me do it!* This is the result of your out of control population growth. Dante Alighieri, the Club of Rome, Steven King, and Dan Brown warned you that things like this would happen if you didn't learn to control your population. All kinds of disasters would happen. This is one more control vector trying to reduce your out-of-control population numbers. Mankind is a curse on this beautiful world and plague is one more way of controlling it."

"Truly are you the Prince of Liars!" Susan said. "You have hated mankind since before the Garden of Eden. You can't stand that God could love a flawed creature better than you. God punished you for attacking mankind when you launched yourself in the Garden of Eden at this poor flawed species incapable of protecting itself from you. Where are your wings, O Serpent? Where is your robes and The Glory of God? You were stripped because you were a flawed bully. Come here, face the truth, and let me heal you."

"Go to Hell, Mort's whore. You should have died of that cancer I put into your spine. I knew you were going to be a curse on me. Just see if you can stop this curse that I have prepared for mankind." Satan waved his hand and disappeared in a cloud of red smoke.

"And there he stands, condemned by his own mouth at last," Susan said. "This is an angelic attacked on mankind and we need angelic help to resolve it. Matthias has a list of angels who have helped him with harvest of souls in the past. He needs your help again. Michael, we need your help training Angels so that they can move as fast as Matthias in releasing souls from plague victims. Uriel we need ideas from you and saints who have worked with plague and Ebola victims when they were on earth. They can help us anticipate the next outbreaks of plague and ways they used to intercept the next wave of infections. We need halfway houses conveniently located for newly released souls where they can rest before being shuttled on to their final heavenly homes. We need Archangels who can stop time while other Angels do collections when they completely run out of time during infection firestorms. The Creator would not have challenged us with this *impossible* task if we do not have a way of dealing with it. The Bible taught me that all things are possible through Christ who strengthens us. Let's get with it people!"

Matthias and the existing angel teams swept into the first plague outbreaks in Asiatic Greece and Constantinople harvesting souls as new teams of Angels and newly arrived Saints were being inoculated and rammed into Michael's speed up boot camp in Heaven. As soon as they graduated they were thrown into the front lines to stomp out new plague outbreaks and cleans ships of rats and fleas before they docked. Other Angels worked with CDC saints ahead of the plague front to spread information on public hygiene and burning of plague victims and their bedding and clothing. Others provide information to doctors on symptoms, expected outbreaks, and medical protection to first responders. The advancing Mongol hordes were using plague victims as biological war weapons when they catapulted diseased bodies into cities under siege in Samarkand and Bagdad, Persia. As new teams of Saints were trained they were thrown into sites beyond the immediate infection sites to other expected sites of infections to prepare them for the onslaught of the disease. Teams were supported by strong-arm bands of Angels to protect the healers from attacks and claims that they were witches, wizards, and others trying to harm rather than protect the people. Miracles and healings of existing disease helped to convince these misguided armies of non-believers. The unbelievers and the lazy were the first victims at the wave front of infection. The intelligent survivors who cleansed their homes and city led the way into the Renaissance as the plague front swept across Italy, southern France, up into Britton, the Netherlands, Germany, and Poland and Russia.

While the waves of plague were dying out, the waves of religious intolerance followed on its heels. A thousand years of biblical silence ended when the printing press made the Bible available to anyone who could read.

Martin Luther challenged the Pope's sale of Indulgences to pay for St. Peter's cathedral setting off the 30-years war between the Catholic Church and its Holy Orders and the Protestant heretics. Now plague and persecutions went hand in hand. Matthias teams had to deal with both religious and infectious deaths, sometimes at the same time. The city of Magdeburg in the German states was nearly wiped off the map by a Catholic-lead siege and plague and other diseases around 1630.

Susan and her team helped to stop the plague in the Lowlands and neighboring France. Matthias final convinced the Brits in London that the repeated waves of Plagues were restarting from rats eating the plague bodies of the nobility buried in Westminster Abbey. Slowly, most of the plague invasion stopped early in the 1500s. But, new waves broke out until the 18th century. The attack on mankind for the moment seemed to have ended, but even more virulent attacks were being prepared.

Chapter Seven
The Holocaust and Hiroshima

"In the twentieth century, the new wave of multiple deaths came from the Great War machines of Europe. A warning of what could happen appeared with the death of two great ocean-going passenger ships. The HMS Titanic was a passenger liner carrying refugees fleeing the threats of war in Central Europe. There was nothing new about war in Europe. France and Germany had invaded each other's territory for fifty years disrupting people lives. The death of the great ship Titanic in 1912 was an apparent accident; two much speed, poor construction, and collision with an iceberg cost 1500 lives due to insufficient lifeboats, mostly of poor people in steerage. But, this was not the end of the problem," Matthias said.

Matthias and Susan appeared on the deck of the Titanic as the great ship was slowly going down nose first as the last of the life boats cast off leaving over half of the passengers and crew on the deck as the lights went out. Matthias raced around the deck releasing souls of men, women, and children. He transferred Susan to one of the half-filled lifeboats, and then went into the freezing water to release souls from those struggling and swimming in the freezing water in floatation belts. By the time he returned for Susan the Archangel was blue with the cold. She touched his arm and they turned onto the road to Raphaella home. She got him into the house as fast as possible and in front of a roaring fire. Matthias stripped off his clothing and wrapped himself in a pile of blankets.

"That was awful," Susan said, "The sound of those poor people screaming and moaning as they saw their sure death coming, even working as fast as you could. Nothing like that can ever be allowed to happen."

"That and worse will happen soon," Matthias said. "World War is coming again. Five years from now, a German submarine will torpedo an American liner, the Lusitania, carrying 1450 passengers and munitions for the British war effort and all will be lost. The ship rolls and will sink so fast that none of the lifeboats will be able to be launched. The ship will sink 50 miles off the Irish coast with no survivors. And it won't be the only ship sunk by submarines during this war with no survivors. Cargo ships running in convoys will be sunk by U-boats off the American coast and at sea in the Atlantic. A few survivors will be rescued, but many more will be lost at sea during this half-century war. And I have to release them all. And the drowning victims are not the only casualties. This is a shooting war with machine guns, poison gas, long range cannons, and area fire-bombardment and dogfights between aircraft."

"In the second half of this terrible conflict, 82 million people will be killed in combat, 6 million Jews will be murdered in gas chambers, and 12 million serfs will starve to death at the hands of the Russian government attempting to free up food for the war effort. I can't imagine that many murders, that many souls to be released," Matthias said shaking his head. "This war will end with the death of three cities: Dresden, Germany by fire-bombing and Hiroshima, and Nagasaki, Japan from the first nuclear bombings. The last two cost the lives of 270,000 people in less than 5 minutes each. Can you imagine releasing souls from all those burn victims in Dresden and Japan or those victims of nuclear blasting and burning? Not all of them are Christians or Jews, but they all bear God's Rhuach seed, that must be recovered. I guess I'll have to learn to harvest Rhuach seed out of the mushroom blast clouds. Victims killed on the battlefield or in the concentration camp gas chambers are a snap compared to victim vaporized in gas clouds. What kind of monsters would do such things?"

Susan said, An American general from their Civil War said that, "*War is Hell!* I believe he was right. When are we leaving?"

"I don't want you on the battle fields. There is no way I can protect you there from poison gas and machine gun bullets," Matthias said. "Early on in the war, you might be able to help the wounded as an "angel of the battlefield," but in the final days you will be more useful helping to direct the angel coalition here in Heaven. You have the organization knowledge and skills to help make it happen here. I am going to have to be moving too fast to keep an eye on you. I want you some place safe where I can come and seek comfort from this horror of the inhumanity of mankind."

Susan found herself dressed in a brown pant uniform with a Red Cross on her sleeve and laced boots on her feet. On her back she wore a knapsack filled with bandages, medications, surgical tools, and a gas mask. She touched Matthias' arm and found themselves in a muddy trench with shells screaming overhead. Above her head she could here the buzz of machine gun bullets and the occasional explosion of mortar shells. She was too busy tending torn bodies and patching up bleeding wounds to worry about her own safety. As soon as she finished patching one body, it was carried off on a stretcher and another took its place. Obviously, someone was triaging the wounded because there was always something she could do for the victim. She prayed with the injured while she patched them up. Occasionally she had to use Raphaella's healing technique to save someone who was sliding away on her from a bleeding body wound.

Suddenly, Matthias was there to grab her in his arms and carry her to the steps of Raphaella's cottage. "Mustard Gas was coming. You have done all you could. You don't need a whiff of mustard to end your day. You were burned out and have had enough. You need to rest." Matthias carried her up to her bedroom, unlaced her boots, and tucked her in. "You have an angel training seminar for young Angels to conduct in the morning. Sleep." He bent over to give her a kiss on the forehead, which was the last thing she remembered.

In the morning, Susan padded out to breakfast in her uniform and thick socks. Matthias set at the table in a Red Cross uniform grey-faced looking exhausted. Susan settled on his lap and kissed him. She held him, whispered in his ear, and wiped the wrinkles from his face as Raphaella had showed her. “Where are we going today?” She asked.

“After I sleep and you conduct your angel-training seminar, we will head to France as the French army collapses under the German blitzkrieg trapping the British army at the Dunkirk beachhead. You can help the survivors get off the beach while I harvest the armored vehicle crews fleeing the on-rushing German tanks. Once we get to England, I'll be harvesting the victims of the bombing Blitz of London and suburban England while you drive an ambulance helping to rescue victims of the bombing. Then you will move to Canterbury when the Germans go after the cathedral with bombing raids.”

Susan found herself in a British nursing uniform again with a Red Cross armband and her medical knapsack. Her ambulance was burning on the side of the road as she walked with troops heading for the beach. Above them she could here the German dive-bombers screaming down on the troops followed by the sound of exploding bombs. Fighter aircraft dove on the fleeing soldiers strafing them with machine guns and cannons. Susan wore a flat helmet that one of her dying patients had forced her to take. When they reached the shore she was placed on one of the three-man fishing boat, which had just reached shore after crossing the English Channel. It was quickly refueled from a tanker and then overloaded with troops carrying their wounded. Susan immediately went to work patching up the wounded while the remaining soldiers were firing at the dive bombers, one of which was hit with rifle fire and crashed into the water, nearly swamping the fishing boat as they were pulling out into the channel. The boat wallowed out into the Channel toward Dover with soldiers everywhere. Susan began to get seasick as the waves hit the side. The troops were all bailing water over the side with their helmets. Suddenly, Matthias was by her side, put her arms around her, and they were on Raphaella's front step.

“Thank God you arrived when you did, I thought I was going to die. I hate being seasick!” Susan said. Raphaella laid her hands along her face, kissed her, and hummed a lullaby to her and her nauseous feeling disappeared as she collapsed.

Susan woke in her bed the next morning, grabbed a shower, and walked out to find a different brown uniform with a Red Cross armband and new army boots on her bed. Heading into the smell of bacon and eggs, she found Matthias eating. "I thought you would want to know that your shipmates all survived to reach England although that trawler ran out of fuel and had to be towed into shore by a private yacht. Those little ships rescued the British Army and saved them to fight again." Matthias said. "The people you treated all lived to return to their families, only to have to survive the bombing of London and the countryside during the Blitz, the Buzz bombs, and eventually the V2 rockets at the end of the War. The RAF planes piloted by many of the soldiers from the beachhead won the air war in the Battle of Britain and the German sea invasion never managed to get a single foot on British soil thanks to the army you helped rescue."

"Today," Matthias said, "You will be driving an ambulance in London rescuing civilians injured by the German bombers attacking the city. Your healing skills will allow you to save many while I am busy releasing the souls of those trapped in the rubble. England never believed that the monster in Germany would attack defenseless civilians. Soon the shoe will be on the other foot as England retaliates against German war production at great loss to the British bomber crews."

"Throughout the war the savagery of the bombing will increase, until the Germans attack the sanctuary city of Canterbury with its great Cathedral, which will be partially destroyed by the bombers. That will lead the Brits to retaliate against civilians by firebombing the museum city of Dresden and, eventually, the capital city of Berlin."

Susan drove her ambulance through the streets saving many injured civilians of Canterbury until her ambulance was destroyed by a falling chimney from the cathedral. She managed to crawl out the back dragging the housewife injured in the destruction of her house with her. "Go on, Ducks," the lady said. "You got me patched up. Now you need to take care of yourself."

Susan limped on a damaged leg holding her broken left arm until Matthias found her and whisked her to Raphaella's home and surgery. The angry Archangel kissed her guest to stop the pain, touched her knee that was screaming, and healed her broken arm with a lullaby. "Mort has got to take better care of you," Raphaella said, "He's going to get you killed. Even he could not fix you then. He may not be able to die, but you can. You may be hard to kill, but you can be utterly destroyed."

"Susan, I am so sorry," Matthias said. "I only saw that falling pile of bricks at the last moment. I could only deflect most of the weight, but I was terrified when the ambulance got smashed. I was amazed when you and Mrs. Brown climbed out of the rear. I have to go deal with the concentration camp victims and Polish intellectual murders. I don't want you around those SS murderers; they are pure, unadulterated evil. If you want, you can go into work with the survivors in the camps after the American troops liberate the camps. Those poor people will really need your healing touch."

So Susan drove a bread, cheese, and milk truck that she had liberated from a German bakery in a nearby village into Buchenwald and began to distribute her stores as she reached out to the poor suffering souls left over from the mercies of the Nazis. Some people she could heal with Raphaella's technique, many other she had to surrender to Matthias' touch. Most brought her to tears as she healed them and fed them until her food was gone. She snapped some picture with her camera. Then she drove her stolen bakery truck to the nearby American camp to load up with more food and chocolate bars. When they argued with her, she showed them pictures from the camp, and they loaded her up with all the rations she needed including two 50-gallon pots of today's stew, then filled the back with fresh baked loaves of bread and wheels of cheese.

Susan headed back to the camp gates now thrown wide open, parked, and threw the truck's back doors open to return to her mission of mercy. She sat with her customers, healing sores on their body, hands, and feet as they pushed food into their mouths. Eventually, the sun went down and the Americans got some lights on. Susan worked as long as she could. When she was ready to collapse, she turned her medical knapsack, her collection of pictures, and her food truck over to a young American Captain with a caduceus pin on his label and shoulder and put her hand on Matthias' arm. She was ready for bed and was sound asleep in is arms when the arrived on the small path before the two-story green cottage.

The next day, Matthias carried her through the air over both Hiroshima and Nagasaki to give her an idea of the devastation caused by nuclear bombing and then flew her over many of the other Japanese cities that had been systematically firebombed. By the end of the war more than nine million Japanese civilians had no homes with winter coming on. Matthias set her down in her WAC uniform with its Red Cross sleeve on the hills around Hiroshima where she immediately began treating burn victims. The people she treated brought to her *the Great Bomb Lady*; this lady had been facing away from the atomic blast wearing a beautiful painted kimono. The blast had burned a negative of the kimono pattern into her back and burned off her hair in the back. She now made her living showing her scars to all who would see the effect of the American Bomb. Many of her burned victims had been pulled out of the city itself and were suffering from radiation burns; many of them were children from area schools. Susan's treated their ulcerated burns and used Raphaella's healing to clean out the radioactive scaring and cancers. There was nothing she could do to bring back their missing parents.

Matthias showed up with good news about his success in recovering God's Rhuach seed out of the mushroom clouds from the nuclear blasts. He had to wait until the boiling temperature cooled as the cloud reached the stratosphere and then was able to scoop Rhuach seed with an attractive net that he had developed with Uriel's, assistance as he moved at the speed of thought. A similar technique worked with victims completely consumed in bombing firestorms in Dresden, Tokyo, Yokohama, and other major industrial cities in Japan. He still had to manually collect souls from badly burned victims as they passed away.

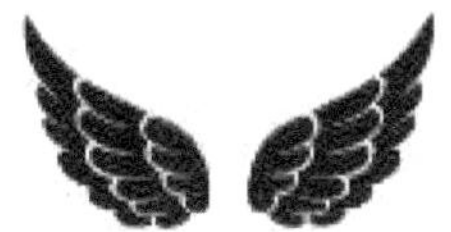

Chapter Eight
The Tribulation Saints

As Matthias and Susan moved into the Twenty-first century, the carnage continued and increased. Muslin terrorist, flying hijacked departing passenger aircraft stolen from nearby airports, attacked the twin towers in New York City and the Pentagon Building in, D.C. Innocent passengers aboard the aircraft died with the terrorist when the gasoline loaded planes smashed into the buildings. Matthias flashed through the planes releasing souls of both passengers and terrorists to carry off to different location. The fourth plane targeted for the White House was taken back by heroic passengers in hand to hand fighting, but crashed in a Pennsylvania field at the cost of all the lives aboard after all had been released by Matthias.

As the buildings burned and people died falling from the roofs and windows, Susan stood on the sidewalk outside as Matthias raced through first the South Tower and then the North Tower releasing souls. Passed by firemen and policemen racing into the burning building, Susan had to run for her life as first the South Tower and then the North Tower crumpled to the ground taking 3,000 victims to their deaths. Amazingly, thousand of people raced for their lives down stairwells and into subway stations to escape. A few people and first responders were miraculously rescued from the fallen debris. Clouds of smoke, flying debris, and sheets of paper showered and smothered first responder, reporters, by-standers, and people fleeing the disaster.

Motor vehicle deaths in America had slowly increase to over fifty thousand a year with thousands more wounded, maimed, and crippled for life on the nations highways. Suddenly after the turn of the millennia, it jumped to nearly seventy thousand with many of the victim among the youngest adults who insisted on playing with cell phones as they drove down the street. Instant communication led to distracted driving led to a terrible rise in horrendous head-on crashes. Matthias found himself rushing down the streets and highways releasing souls of teenage and twenty-year old drivers barely old enough to get a driver's license. At the same time, handgun murders increased every evening in the cities as right-to-carry laws proliferated. America's fascination with guns and cars led to a plague of nationwide drive-by shootouts as the insanity rate soared. Susan watched with horror as Matthias was crushed with the rising wave of children dying in two tons of twisted luxury metal holding their cell phones in their hand containing their last text message to friends.

"That's enough," Susan said, "We are going home. You are going to collapse if you keep pushing yourself like this. As you're doctor, I am order a twenty-four hour period of R&R. You need a break from this insanity. We need to talk. We can send in the angel crews we have trained to take care of these idiots." Putting her hand on Matthias' arm she sent them to the green colonial two-story house on the pathway in heaven." Is there any end to this self-inflicted suicide epidemic?" Susan asked

"Yes," Matthias said as Susan sat on his lap slowly rubbing his temples and the back of his neck, while she hummed Raphaella's lullaby. "Finally, gun deaths will plummeted as the Wild West laws storm through State Senates a crossed the U.S. barring open-right-to-carry as people learned to keep their weapons locked up at home or else face seizure and arrest. ARA and gun manufacturer's lobbyists will be banned from state and federal government facilities as taxes on new handguns soared. Sales of automatic weapons will be banned and outlawed in the U.S. The idea that these war weapons were *hunting weapons* was finally dismissed as totally ridiculous, as it always had been. Sales of any weapon led to serious convictions of the distributors as accessory before the fact, if the federally registered weapons were used in murders or robberies leading to deaths. Possession of a stolen handgun or a Saturday Night Special quickly led to seizure and automatic jail time."

"Car deaths begin to creep down as the diving license age increased to thirty and convictions on distracted drivers rose as accidents with a cell phone in the car automatically lead to jail time, heavy fines, and lifetime ban on cell phone ownership. Second conviction led to much harsher sentences. Finally, people learned the lesson of distracted driving and began to use ride sharing. They brought their cell phones with them, but left them in their pockets or purses. They learned that if the phone rings, they don't have to answer it! The caller can always leave a message. No answered message is worth a life."

"Quit talking! You are stuck on fast forward," Susan, said leaning forward to kiss the Archangel. "Rest. Recuperate. Sleep. Recover. Sleep!" She snuggled next to Matthias in his bed. "What am I going to do with you?" She whispered, "You are an impossible choice! I can't fall in love with a being made only of energy. "Dumb, Susan, you always make such impossible choices!" She rollover next to Matthias and went to sleep.

In the morning, Matthias staggered into the kitchen to find Susan and Raphaella around the table in head to head conversation. "What's going on," he said as he grabbed his cup of coffee and drank it black.

"Nothing," Susan replied. "We are just having some girl talk. Raphaella is my confessor. I need to have someone to go to also. What's on the agenda for today?"

"Today we are headed for an encounter with the Beast from the Sea and to collect souls from the tribulation saints." Matthias said. "New Christians still find their way to Jeshua even after the church saints were collected. The anti-Christ followers along with the remaining un-converted Jews will target them. They are the new martyrs who are destined to dwell with Jeshua in his millennial kingdom."

"Wrong, This morning you have an appointment with the boss. Prince Lucifer has filed a grievance with the boss against Susan claiming that she has interfered with his administrative duty on Earth.

He has named Dr. Matthias Mort Samael as her administrative Archangel for the grievance committee meeting. You will have to handle this before you can return to your angelic duties. Sorry," said Raphaella with a grin.

"A grievance? What are we supposed to be a union? The United Brotherhood of Seraphs, Cherubim, and attending Angels? That's crazy," Samael said.

"God said that you are to take care of this," Raphaella said with a grin. "Jeshua will be setting in judgment, sort of practice for the White Throne judgment at the end of the Age."

The Court of Judgment was held on the rolling green lawn behind Raphaella and Uriel's house. Jeshua sat in a white-painted lawn chair and tapped a gavel on the armrest. The Archangel Michael rose and said, "Court is in session to hear Lucifer's charges against the angel Susan for interfering with his administrative duties on earth. You may inform the court of the specifics of your charges, Lucifer."

Satan rose and said, "On the 22nd. of March in 29 A.D. I appeared before the Roman Centurion in charge of the execution of a criminal at four o'clock in the afternoon in Jerusalem and presented him with documentation from the High Priest Caiaphas releasing the body of the deceased to me for burial. As you know the bodies of dead criminals are usually thrown in the waste dump or left to rot on their cross. The High Priest did not want the sight of rotting bodies to disturb pilgrims during the celebration of the Passover holy days."

"And why exactly did the High Priest select you for such a mission?" Jeshua asked.

"Because he knew that I had been appointed by Yahweh to oversee action on earth. The criminal on the cross had been condemned by the Sanhedrin as a heretic disturbing the People and Caiaphas wanted him disposed of once and for all."

"What stopped you from collecting the body?" Michael asked.

"That female right there who works for Archangel Mort Samael appeared, insulted me, and prevented me from approaching the Centurion in charge at the moment of death. She engaged me in conversation and tried to use one of Raphaella's magical techniques to stop my performance of my assigned duties. A mortal named Josephus of Arimathea arrived with a document from Proconsul Pilate releasing the body to him. I was prevented from doing my assigned duty and I want her punished for her action."

"Defense," Said Jeshua. "How do you respond?"

"If I may, your Holiness," said Susan. "As usual, Satan has twisted his facts. First, I am not an angel. I am a human being. I do not report to Dr. Samael. I am a hired consulting psychiatrist engaged by Samael to travel with him. Because I am not an angel assigned to report to Dr. Samael, I am not subject to censure by this court. As long as we are clarify facts, perhaps we should ask this snake exactly what he planned to do with your body once he had it."

Satan's only answer was a puff of smoke as Lucifer left the courtroom in a rage.

"I guess this trial is dismissed. What exactly do you think he was going to do with my body once he had it?"

"Probably prevent your resurrection. Possibly use it to reanimate as the anti-Christ. That is what his lieutenant Abaddon said they were going to do with it before I stopped him.

That's probably why Satan disappeared before he had to answer that question," said Susan.

"Court dismissed. Well that was interesting. Feel free to return to your work. Good to see you again Susan. Good job." Jeshua disappeared.

* * * *

"What are we doing today?" Susan asked.

"Today we will be collecting the souls of the church and tribulation saints. If you remember your reading of 1Thessalonians, Daniel, and Revelation, we are rapidly approaching the Second Coming of The Messiah. First the dead in Christ will arise and then the Church will rise to meet Jeshua in the cloud of witnesses. This fourteen-year period of terrible testing will occur on earth while the Third Temple is built under the protection of the Beast from the Sea, desecrated, and taking over by the Anti-Christ. Many will die, both those who serve Jeshua, and those who still not made the decision. The believers in the Anti-Christ must all be marked with his sign, 666. Anyone who is not marked is considered rebels. They may not shop or buy anything for sustaining life without the beast's mark. If arrested they will be executed."

"All of the God-marked who are killed must be collected for they have the Rhuach. Many will come to believe in Jeshua during this time of tribulation. The church may be gone, but the Bible remains. Many of these tribulation saints will have relatives, who have accepted Jeshua, shared the Good News, and have passed on. Many will received the word from the 144,000 Jewish evangelicals commissioned and protected by God with the sign of Cain. They all must be freed at the second coming of Jeshua, the Battle of Armageddon, and the fall of the Anti-Christ, the False Prophet, and Satan into the pit in chains. Jeshua will cleans the Temple as the seat of his millennial kingdom where he will rule over his tribulation saint for one thousand years before the final judgment."

Susan was dressed in a camouflage pantsuit that Samael had provided, a Boston Strong T-shirt, combat boots, and a Boston Red Sox's baseball cap, with her Red Cross band on her arm. She found herself in the rush-hour opening of the graves of the deceased believers and then the soul collection of the living church members. She occasional had a glimpse of Matthias as he released souls of the children of God at the speed of thought. Clouds of Angels and Saints swooped in to gather the souls to lead them into Heaven. Demons gathered to block the release of souls and the angelic collection. Susan in the arms of a newly trained angel charged into the demons to touch them with her healing touch to protect the newly released souls.

Suddenly, Susan found herself surrounded by angels and saints on horses dressed in formal wedding clothing surrounding Jeshua on a horse with blood up to its belly. They charged into the chaos of the soul collection, scattered the demon hoards, and gathered the released souls into convoys to be lead into Heaven.

A moment later, Matthias appeared at her side, put her hand on his arm, and jumped onto the path leading to Raphaella's colonial house. "Time for a break," he said. "Thank heavens for the experience of gathering the Black Plague victims. I never would have been able to handle this load amidst the demonic hoard. I did answer one question that has haunted Heaven. Demons, and I assume angels do not have God's Rhuach. When you touch the spot on their neck, the souls released, but does not have a Pearl of great value."

"Were are we going?" Susan asked.

"Home to the cottage for a nap. I am flat burned to a cinder. We are going to sleep and prepare us for the harvest of the tribulation saints. This collection has been a snap compared to what we will face in land of the anti-Christ. Those saints have faced torture, torment, and beheadings. It is not going to be pretty. You might want to sit this one out."

"Wither thou go, I will go. This place sounds like it's going to be the very place you will need me most," Susan said collapsing on her bed.

Breakfast with Raphaella was quiet with coffee and fresh baked rolls. Matthias came in and went over to the icebox looking for orange juice and a glass of milk. Raphaella looked at Samael, smiled, and said, "Do you want me to fix you some ham and eggs?"

"No, I'd just throw it up. This is a really bad time coming up and I just have to get through it. This guy Sheppard, the antichrist, is Satan on steroids. After he was attacked by that Muslim with a sword, had his head split from crown to his chin, and then was healed by his false prophet, he has become totally irrational. He will do anything to get people to believe in him and if you don't believe he has no place for you in his world. And if you don't believe, he has no compunction about removing you from his world. He has let non-believers starve to death in his prisons: men, women, and children. He has now set up guillotines throughout his kingdoms and is threatening to get rid of non-believers with them: men, women, and children. He is hanging convicted felons up on meat hooks to die in their cells like Hitler did. Few people realize that Hitler had 16,000 people killed with the guillotine in the last years of his reign of terror. He is truly a monster. Can you conceive of a child beheaded on one of those things?" Mort asked.

"I have no interest in thinking of such a thing," said Susan. "Why would God allow such a monster to live? Even with free will, what can such monsters add to God's world? Ugh!"

"I don't try to know God's will. Have you finished eating, we need to go and get this over?" Matthias said."

"I'm ready. Where are we going?"

"Jerusalem again, but in your future. The Tribulation saints are dying all over the world, but they are being collected by my trained death Angels. But the anti-Christ is centering his show trials in the Holy City where he has his guillotine set up. He also has a TV broadcast system set up so that he can broadcast his show executions worldwide in living color to entertain his followers. It is getting harder and harder to find victims. They have to go outside Jerusalem to find underground Tribulation Saints. The locals have burrowed deep into the Temple Mount and Old City and are very careful not to expose themselves to the anti-Christ's spies and Satan's demons." Matthias said. "I will put you down in a safe house while I do my collections. You can help them with their illnesses, since they have no access to hospitals or doctors. I wish I could show you the Holy sites, but it would expose you to Sheppard's spies."

Susan settled in to work in an underground Kibbutz with a nice Jewish family and treated any one who was brought to her. Suddenly the door was broken down and a demon lunged through the doorway. "I've got the bitch. Get the others before they get away." Susan swung her medical bag to trip three of his cohort and stabbed the thing holding her wrist with a scapula. “You'll die for that, bitch. The boss has been looking for you for a week.” The demon trailing blood pouring down his chest hit Susan hard in the face and she remembered nothing more.

When she awoke she was next in line before the steps to the guillotine. The sound of the blade dropping ended with a sickening crunch as the crowd cheered and shouted in encouragement. “Next,” called the executioner in a black hood. A demon on each arm yanked her up the steps and dragged her to the stocks under the blade. They forced her to her knees, locked her neck in the stocks, as she heard the blade being cranked back in to position. “I have so been looking forward to this,” came Satan's voice from under the black hood and Susan heard the trigger release snap open and the blade swish down. Susan heard Matthias' voice behind her say, “Susan, my God!” and felt her neck touched from behind her. She felt Matthias gather her in his arm as they soared into the air as she looked down on her headless body kicking in the bloody stocks. That was the last thing she remembered for a long time.

* * * *

She awoke wondering why there was no pain. She was in a soft bed; the ceiling was the one in Raphaella's house. She reached around to feel the back of her neck, but there was no wound that she could feel. Matthias was sitting by her bed and took her hand. “Susan, I am so sorry! I screwed up. I left you alone too long and that snake's minions found you before I could get to you. He rushed you straight to the guillotine before I could rescue you. The blade was on its way down when I got there at the speed of thought. The only thing I could do was to release your soul and race you to Heaven. I demanded and got a resurrection body for you. I am so sorry. It was all I could do. I broke my promise to you that I would take you back to your office if you ever wanted out.”

“Wait, wait,” Susan said, “Go back and unpack that a little. What happened?”

“Satan ambushed you. He filled Jerusalem with his demons, all with picture and descriptions of you. They have been waiting for you for a week. I walked right into the trap. They grabbed you before I realized what was happening. They rushed you right up to your execution. All I could do was rush your soul spirit out of there before Satan knew what was happening. He thinks you are dead.” Matthias said.

“Well am I dead or aren't I?” Susan asked.

“You are and you aren't. It is hard to explain. When we got to Heaven, I confronted Jeshua, and demanded a resurrection body for you because it was my fault that you had died. I threatened to quit on the spot if you were not restored immediately. Jeshua read your soul and agreed with me. Now you have to understand that this is not your personal resurrection body. It is an off-the-shelf model. You will be more of an Amazon in this body, almost six-foot tall. I'm sorry this was a rush job. You are not in a body of flesh and blood; this one is made of energy and spirit. It will not age, your body is immortal, it contains your Pearl, but there is no scarlet release button on the back of your neck. We won't have to be afraid that Satan will be able to hurt you ever again. Nor the plague, not cancer, or any other illness, not even a cold. Your resurrection body is like mine. I am sorry I couldn't do better for you.”

“Matthias, you idiot. Shut up! This body is wonderful. I feel great, full of energy, and ready to go. Let's go find that idiot Satan so I can pound him senseless for pulling that sneaky trick. Come here and give me a kiss,” Susan said. “This is great. I love this body. I've always been such a shrimp. Look at me! I'm gorgeous.” Susan jumped out of bed and posed in front of the mirror. “I always wanted to be a red head, but I was always afraid of the pain of getting a dye job. This is natural,” she said looking down with another blush.

“Susan, you had better gets some clothing on,” Matthias gasped.

Susan looked at what she wasn’t wearing and blushed down to her toes. Matthias quickly dressed her in panties, jeans, a Mickey

Mouse T-shirt, and her tan half boots that had stretched to fit her feet. “Let's go get some breakfast, I'm starved. Is Raphaella here?” she asked. Susan asked Raphaella for a thin red ribbon to tie around her neck. “The execution ribbon is an old French tradition to symbolize sympathy for someone executed on the guillotine,” Susan said will a grin. “Sort of gallows humor.”

Together Susan and Matthias went through the world of the anti-Christ gathering souls for the Millennial Kingdom and stepping forward past the second coming of the Christ. They saw him touch down on the Mount of Olives just as he had left on Ascension Day. They saw an earthquake rip the mountain apart and move the pieces North and South opening the Valley of Jehoshaphat so that the water from under the temple could run down the River of Deliverance to sweeten the Dead Sea. They deposited the newly liberated souls into new bodies in the restored and lifted up Jerusalem of Jeshua's millennial kingdom.

On one trip back while they watched, they saw Jeshua ride through the bricked up entrance of the Beautiful Gate and shatter the double gate of the Eastern wall of the Temple. The Beast from the Sea, the Beast from the Land, and the indwelling Satan and their army tried to stop the Risen Christ on his bloody horse, but all he did was point at them and spoke the Word of God and they were blasted away. Sheppard, the anti-Christ, with his head ripped open again, and the false prophet were thrown into the burning pit, as was a shriveled Satan wrapped in chains.

Satan was sentenced to stay there for a thousand years. Susan cheered his fall, although she wished she could have been allowed to kick him into the flames.

With both beasts and their master thrown into the flames, their followers were left scattered and leaderless. When the angelic host found those with the mark of the beast, they were seized, examined by the Messiah, and if they were guilt of crimes against the followers of Jeshua, they were cast into the flames to await their final judgment. Matthias and Susan flashed through the seven years of the Beast's rule looking for those behead, burned, and killed in other exotic manners, to release their souls, and gather them up to escort them to Jeshua kingdom. Eventually all the Saint's souls, were collect and home with Jeshua for a thousand years.

When finally, the ingathering of souls was complete, Susan and Matthias retired to the green colonial two-story house on the path in Heaven to join Raphaella, Uriel, and Michael for supper. Susan asked, “Are we done? Is your collection assignment over?”

“No,” Dr. Samael said. “I have one final assignment before I can retire. A time is coming when everyone most stand before judgment. Everything they have done must be reviewed, before a new heaven and a new earth is created. Death will be done away with. Then and only thing can I give up by job.”

“What will you do when you have worked your way out of a job?” Raphaella asked.

“I have no idea,” said Matthias, “what God’s retirement assignment will be. But, I am sure of one thing, he will have a plan.”

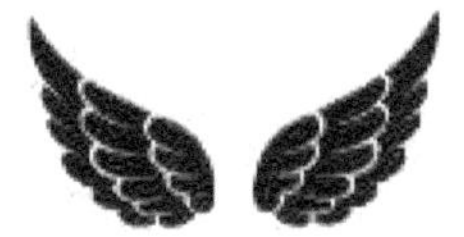

Chapter Nine
The End of Time

The morning dawned bright and shining in the Kidron Valley east of the walls of the Jerusalem Temple. The doublewide step with pools on the side for purification of pilgrims has been restored. The doublewide Beautiful Gate had been replaced in the wall leading to the Court of The Gentiles. At the foot of the steps in the mouth of Jehoshaphat Valley sat the Throne of Judgment covered in pillows and white silk cloth. Across the valley the North Mount of Olives was covered with Tribulation Saints out of Jeshua's city. In the same way, the believers who had survived persecution by the anti-Christ, covered the slopes of the South Mount of Olives and the Garden of Gethsemane The melted statue of the Desecrating Abomination had been thrown into the Hinnom Valley garbage dump broken into tiny pieces. Giant TV screens hung in the air over the Kidron Valley so that the crowds on the hills could see the Judgment of the Ages.

Precisely at eight o'clock Gabriella blew her trumpet and the recording Archangel Jeremiel announced the Judgment of the Lord. In a moment the valleys were filled with the angelic host and Satan's demonic servants extending back into Heaven. Before Jeshua's throne a pit filled with flames opened. The host knelt before the Lord and acknowledged Jeshua as Lord. The Angel of the Books read the Angelic Covenant. The first angel judged was Lucifer, who had been chained in the pit for a thousand years, had been released, and gone to the north to raise the forces of Gog and Magog to attack the Holy City. God had rained fire down on them and stopped them in an instant. Now a charred Satan in chains stood before Jeshua, and was cast into the furnace with the anti-Christ, the false prophet. His fallen-angel demonic host followed them as each was judged, and sent into the pit to joined Prince Lucifer who had led them into rebellion against God.

The remaining angels were judged and dismissed into Heaven to prepare it for the descent of the Heavenly City. A few Angels failed the judgment when secret sins were uncovered and they followed their fallen brothers into the pit. Next, the valleys were filled with humans of all races, creeds, and colors who all bowed their knees and acknowledge Jeshua as Lord. The Archangel of the Books read the Covenants made with Moses, Isaiah, Jeremiah, Muhammad and the Book of Revelation of the Risen Christ. Time had come for the separation of the sheep and the goats described in the Book of Mathew. Dr. Matthias Mort Samael joined the Lord for his last action as the Archangel of Death. As each human was judged his soul was released by a touch on the back of his neck. If they passed the judgment and their names were in both the Book of the Life and the Book of the Lamb, they joined the Tribulation Saints on the Mounts of Olives. If their names were only in the Book of Life, their actions and their hearts were judge by Jeshua from his throne. Those whose actions and minds served the Lord were sent to the Mounts of Olives to join the Saints. They immediately were transformed into their resurrection bodies.

If they failed the Lord's testing, they were sent into the pit for eternity, forever separated from the Lord. Those whose names were in neither the Book of the Lamb or the Book of Life immediately faced the Second Death. Their pearls were ripped out, collected, and their bodies were cast into the fiery pit to be instantly destroyed. Hitler, the Great Khan, Stalin, a collection of Caesars, and barbarian leaders provided a colorful fireworks show as they flashed into nothingness. Their Pearls of great value were collected for cleansing before they went into the pit of separation. A few of the human monsters such as Nero, Caligula, Hitler, Stalin and their crew of diseased followers names were in neither book. Matthias touched their necks, gathered their diseased pearls and their souls were extinguished in a flash of intense pain of the second death. Last of all to go into the pit of punishment were Death and Hades where they flashed into nothingness. Death on earth, which had cursed the Earth since the fall in the Garden of Eden, was no more.

Matthias and Susan were waved into the Garden of Gethsemane and the pit was closed. Jeshua said, "The time has come for the healing of the Earth. Step side ways into Heaven while the Earth is renewed." In a moment the Earth began to be cleansed and renewed. Oceans were emptied as the windows of heaven were closed and the vaults of Heaven opened to take in all the living water. The low places were filled as the hills were leveled. The mounts of Zion and Moriah were lifted up, and the shining city came down to rest on the new Mount of the Lord with the River of Life streaming out from under the Thrones of God and the Lamb to cleanse the Salt Sea. The City of God stretch 1500 miles in all direction upon the Mount of The New Jerusalem.

The group with Drs. Susan and Matthias Samuel poured back into the new city. They all had addresses to their new palaces in God's great city, for the city was now 1500 miles high. God was busy creating a new Heaven, a place of exploration and inventions, a place where people could grow and learn to network, and love others.

Matthias approached Susan and said, “Where do you want to go? I can take you back home, to your office and practice. Perhaps you would prefer the millennial kingdom with its Tribulation Saints, babies, and medical practice. Or we can stay here in the New Jerusalem. Where do you want to go?”

“Where are you going? What new assignment has God given you? What did he say to you when he called you before him?” Susan asked.

“He said, *well done good and faithful servant. I knew I could trust you to figure out the impossible assignment I gave you. I am glad you sought out a true servant-companion. Keep Susan close. We need her with you. She is a true servant of mine.*”

“Wherever you are going, I am going.” Susan said with a blush at the compliment from All-mighty God.

"Jeshua told me he wants me to be a troubleshooter for the kingdom. He said as long as mankind has free will, there would be problems to be solved. My job is to help them sort out their problems and help put their feet back on God's path. He also told me something else. I am supposed to go, multiply, and be fruitful. I guess I am suppose to create a job training program or something like that," Matthias said. "I guess it goes with the new name. Matthias means *Gift of God.* Mort has no meaning in this world. Samuel means *Name of God.* It's a lot better than Samael, which meant *Venom of God.* Dr. Matthias Samuel, what do you think?"

"We are a nice team, my love. What God is telling you is that you need to go, multiply, and be fruitful. We need to go and have babies. Dr. Susan Maria Samuel, it has a nice ring to it, doesn't it? Can an archangel have babies with a resurrection human? I don't know. I asked Raphaella and she doesn't know either, but she and Uriel are expecting to be fruitful and multiply too. The only way we can find out is to try and put the results in God's hands. Even with less pain in childbirth, New Jerusalem is going to need a licensed mid-wife and psychiatrist. I love you. I want to continue to be your partner. Where you go, I will go with you. Grow our own team. What do you think?"

"It sounds like an excellent idea. I love you Susan. I want to go with you, multiple with you, and be fruitful with you. I respect your mind, your courage, your quick wit, and your sense of humor, your sexy body, and your beautiful Pearl of great value. I want to have a baby girl just like you and a son that can move faster than thought. Thou are God," said Matthias.

The End

About the Author

Dr. McMaster has a PhD in organic chemistry, was a technical instrument Salesman, and has taught Bible studies for 25 years and HPLC courses for 10 yrs. at U.MO-St. Louis, he has 4 instrument text books published, a pair of WW 2 biographies, and numerous science fiction, juvenile adventures in another dimension,

www.ingramcontent.com/pod-product-compliance
Lightning Source LLC
Chambersburg PA
CBHW030414310726
48979CB00002B/415
* 9 7 8 1 9 6 1 6 7 7 5 8 6 *